A DANCE WITH DEATH

An Arianna Archer murder mystery

KAREN BERG-RAFTAKIS

DEDICATION

This book is dedicated to my daughter, Alexandra Maria Raftakis and to my grandmother, Josephine De Luca La Paglia.

ACKNOWLEDGMENTS

Thank you to all the people who bought my first book and/or provided support and encouragement after it was published. The whole process was a huge learning experience for me and I appreciate everyone who took a part in it.

Thank you Allen for looking over the various versions of this book and providing numerous helpful suggestions.

Thank you Mom for reading the rough draft and giving me your opinion so quickly.

I also want to thank those who have graced me with their spiritual support, love and encouragement over the years, including, but not limited to: Faye R., Gloria K., Mary C., Jay M., Lyn J., Susanne D., the "Open Minds for ACIM and NTI" Facebook page and "Awakening Together" communities, and especially Dov F., who provides a wonderful forum with ACIM Gather/Awakening Together Radio where I, along with many others, have shared, taught, learned and loved together.

Other Books by Karen Berg-Raftakis

Murder on the Church Council: An Arianna Archer murder mystery

TABLE OF CONTENTS

CAST OF CHARACTERS

Arianna Archer - Amateur detective/TV and mystery fanatic, who gets to test her investigative skills when a case, unexpectedly, falls into her lap.

Sandra Archer - Arianna's tightly wound, conservative mother and, more often than not, thorn in her side.

Mike Stevenson - Chief of the Meadowville Police Department and Arianna's on-again, off-again boyfriend.

Sallie Rigelli - Promiscuous friend of Arianna's, who allegedly possesses "The Gift" of intuition.

Phil La Paglia - Silver-haired, successful man in his fifties, who takes a liking to Arianna.

Arlene La Paglia - Wealthy, classy and beautiful ex-wife of Phil.

Paula La Paglia - Plain-looking and morose daughter of Phil and Arlene.

Stanley Carter - Slow and elderly bartender at the St. Francis Singles Dance.

Sarah Brewster - Strong and capable widow in charge of all the Singles Dances.

"The Ladies"
Camille Ciccone - Strange and unfriendly, she's a regular at the Dances.
Esther Sullivan - Unhappily divorced woman with a chip on her shoulder.
Rachel Gordon - Single lady in her sixties, who doesn't seem to have much to say.

Chapter One - Invitation

Arianna Archer was at home, in an average-sized house, built in the early 1900's in Meadowville, Illinois. Meadowville was a moderately small, middle-class suburb of Chicago, but it contained many churches, parks, stores, and a variety of houses from small, two-bedroom bungalows, to larger, four to five bedroom Victorians. She was sitting on her queen-sized bed with lilac patterned comforter, sheets, and pillows, taking off her clunky black waitress shoes, and rubbing her left foot ruefully. Her bedroom was moderately-sized, containing a bigger than average closet, a rocking chair that once belonged to her great grandmother, and one antique dresser. It also contained one big walnut bookcase filled with murder mysteries; which included the entire Agatha Christie collection and rows and rows of TV show DVDs.

Arianna was a self-avowed book, specifically mysteries, and television addict. When meeting her for the first time, most people came away with the impression that she was very intelligent, when in fact, she'd even tell you herself, she was actually no smarter than the average Joe. However, she read so much and watched so much TV that she basically knew at LEAST a little about everything, or so she thought. The old axiom, "Jack of all trades, master of none" fit her to a tee, but knowing a little bit about everything came in quite handy for her in the past. Unfortunately, the people closest to her didn't realize or appreciate this gift as much as she did.

Arianna's father died several years ago, but she and her dad always had a very close relationship. Whenever they were fed up with being nagged and pestered by their mother, they would often retire to their basement together and watch TV. John Archer had been much older than her mother and had died in his sleep several years ago. As far as she knew, her mother had not dated anyone seriously since then. Arianna and her father especially loved watching shows like <u>Murder She Wrote</u>. Arianna always felt; however, that there really weren't any great whodunnits on the air, where the audience had to guess who the culprit is. She hated TV shows that told you who the killer is at the beginning, like <u>Columbo</u>. Where's the fun in that? She'd wonder to herself. That's why she preferred shows like <u>The Mentalist</u> over <u>Criminal Minds</u> which, beginning last week, she didn't watch anymore due to all the violence. She had grown tired of having to always forward over the serial killer scenes.

However, <u>The Mentalist</u> was no longer a show she watched either, solely because of the fact that the identity of "Red John" (an unknown serial killer who had numerous victims over the six seasons the show was on the air) was revealed to be somebody that made absolutely no sense at all to the TV viewers. Arianna took it upon herself, of course, to write a livid letter to the producers and writers of the show, ending her diatribe with, "<u>The Mentalist</u> is dead to me!!!"

Arianna felt she'd be a much better writer than those working in Hollywood today. *Most of the writing is so horrible, if only I could live in Los Angeles and write for a hit TV show,* she'd often think to herself. Arianna also believed she'd have made an awesome actress, and/or rock-n-roll singer. Unfortunately, at least in regards to her singing talent, Arianna was deluded. She was actually tone deaf and under the illusion that her voice was both pleasant and in tune. This was not the case. In fact, her family couldn't even tolerate her singing in the shower, so when they renovated their bathroom years ago, they made sure the walls were soundproofed.

God, do I hate this. Arianna's unemployment was due to run out in a month, and even though she still couldn't find a full time job, her divorced ex-boyfriend Mike Stevenson, Chief of the Meadowville Police Department, managed to get her a part-time job waitressing, a few months ago at Sandy's Diner. Being the Chief of Police, Mike knew and had good relations with practically every shop and restaurant owner in town. Sandy's Diner was a local establishment known for their 1950's decor and wise-cracking waitresses. Arianna had already been talked to twice for being too cocky, which was saying a lot, since the waitresses there were known for being beyond rude. Once, she told a woman who couldn't control her five bratty kids, "You know, there IS something called The Pill." and the other time she got in trouble, was when she told a sleazy guy who was hitting on her, "You better cut it out, or my boyfriend will chop your *juevos rancheros* off!" The boss, Pete, had told her, in no uncertain terms, one more strike and she was out. Despite the glamorous portrayal of waitresses on the

TV series <u>Alice</u>, it was surprisingly anything but, and her poor feet were killing her. Arianna was used to waitressing, because she had to do it during college, but she was thirty-six years old now and it had lost all its allure.

Arianna was not in a good mood. She was so desperate to quit waitressing, that a few weeks ago she had even tried browbeating Mike into marrying her. She was only half-serious, but still became offended when he said no to her, supposedly because he believed that she'd regret it later, he told her. Mike had also suggested last year, after she had solved two murders at St. James Christian Church, that she could perhaps become a consultant for the police department but, to Arianna's dismay, hadn't taken that idea any further. Her house phone suddenly rang, scaring the crap out of her. *Dammit, I thought I turned the ringer down.*

"Yeah?" Arianna grumpily answered.

"Arianna, could you please answer the phone like a lady, and not like a rude truck driver?" Figures, she thought, only my mother insists on calling me through the landline, instead of entering the twenty-first century and ringing my cell.

"What do you want Mother? I've just got home and I'm exhausted," she answered sharply. Her mother, Sandra Archer, was a blond, blue-eyed, handsome woman in her sixties. She was well-mannered and always concerned with appearances, the exact opposite of her oldest daughter.

"I wanted to let you know, tomorrow night I am going to the Singles Dance at St. Francis Church on Narragansett."

"So?" Arianna responded impatiently.

"Well, I thought you might want to come along."

Arianna was just about to say no, as she usually did to her mother's invitations, but this time she hesitated. She was off work tomorrow night. Maybe she'd be able to score some rich guy there and be a lady of leisure for the rest of her life, she thought. If she soaked her feet in Epsom salts tonight, they should be okay for dancing tomorrow night, she figured. She took a deep breath. "Sure," she replied.

Sandra, despite being in shock that her daughter finally said yes to one of her invitations, immediately replied, "Great, I'll pick you up at 7:30 tomorrow evening."

"OK, see you then." Arianna hung up the phone.

Her two long-haired black cats, Tony and Carmela, both jumped on the bed at the same time. "Oh babies," she cooed, "I love you two so much." She sighed and nuzzled her face into their fur. "You always make me feel better, don't you?" They both butted her stomach with their heads in response.

She got up and grabbed the large plastic container, now dubbed, the "Epsom salts bowl", and filled it with warm water from her bathroom sink. She held on to it gingerly, but the water still splashed over the sides, as she walked into her bedroom. "Dammit!" Arianna said, irritated. She sat down at the edge of the bed, rolled down her pantyhose, threw them on the floor, and submerged both feet in the water. "Ahh," Arianna said aloud, "this feels good." She sat there content for a couple of minutes, until she remembered she agreed to go out with her mother the following night, and even worse, her mother would be driving. *Oh, what have I gotten myself into?* She stood up, walked into her modest kitchen, and pulled a bottle of chilled wine from the refrigerator. She grabbed a glass from the cupboard, and guzzled down a glassful of *Asti Spumanti*, then another, and another...

The next morning, Arianna woke to the sound of her cell phone blasting, "I'm Too Sexy" by Right Said Fred. "Hello?" she mumbled sleepily, as she hit the speaker phone button.

"Well, good morning Sunshine!" Mike Stevenson's voice came roaring over the phone.

"Oh my God, why are you screaming?" she asked wincing, as she covered her ears with both hands and slowly sat up in bed.

"Oh, did you happen to drink a little last night?" he shouted even louder.

"Geez Louise, Mike, what do you want?" she asked, exasperated.

"Since you're not working tonight, I was just checking to see if you want any company later."

"I have other plans," Arianna smugly told him.

"Oh," Mike asked, his interest piqued, "more important than *moi*?"

"Yes, why should I spend any time with you anyway? You were the one who spurned MY marriage proposal. I am going to attend a St. Francis Singles Dance with my mother."

"In response to your stupid question, the ONLY reason you wanted to marry me was for my vast fortune," he said, pretending to be deeply offended. "Also, are you actually going to a dance with Sandra?" he asked incredulously.

"OK, in response to your stupid response to my intelligent question, WHAT vast fortune? You're a cop. Secondly, yes I am going with my mother. Who knows? Maybe I'll even meet the man of my dreams," she retorted.

"Well, good luck with that," Mike replied. "I'll let you go now, I can't afford to waste any more time talking with you, I have an entire village to save," he said dramatically.

"Later." Arianna ended the call.

Arianna and Mike had what you'd call a consistent on-again, off-again relationship. They would date a few months, and according to Arianna, Mike would inevitably start acting clingy and possessive, and so Arianna would ask him to give her some space. Because his ego was taking a beating, he'd get mad at her and deliberately start acting obnoxious. Of course, she'd have no choice BUT to break up with him. Both of them had dated other people, but Mike hadn't had any long-term relationships, since his divorce twenty years ago, except for Arianna. Prior to Mike meeting Arianna, he dated quite a few women after his divorce, mainly to get over the pain, but none of the relationships were of any significance. During the several break-ups Mike and Arianna had over the years, Arianna had a couple of semi-serious relationships, which lasted a year or so, but none of them stuck. Mike dated as well, but he knew his heart wasn't really into it. So for better or for worse, they kept going back to each other. Her mother and sister Emily were aware that Arianna and Mike had dated, but for the last several years, they had both agreed to keep them out of the loop when it came to their relationship. The couple, especially Arianna, very much valued their privacy. She didn't need her mother and sister constantly asking her when she was going to marry Mike or pressuring Mike to ask her to marry him. She had enough issues to deal with.

The reason Mike and Arianna didn't consider themselves a couple right now, was because a few months ago Mike had asked her to move in with him, and she refused. The reasons, she cited, were that she loved her house and she seriously didn't know if she could live with a man 24/7, without wanting to kill him in his sleep. He, of course, immediately became upset and had shut her out completely for weeks. They had recently moved past all that and had been talking to each other over the past month, but their relationship hadn't progressed much past the "friends" level yet.

One hour before her mother was due to pick her up, she stood staring into her closet. Arianna, 5'10", with long natural blond hair, green eyes, and possessing what she'd like to think of as a voluptuous figure, was greatly distraught. All of the outfits she had thought about wearing that night were too tight. "Buggers!" she cried out loud. *I can't understand it, how could I have gained so much weight, so fast?* Arianna was conveniently forgetting all of the Girl Scout cookies and pints of chocolate ice cream she had devoured, since the company she worked for, a book distribution firm, had laid her off over a year ago. Incidentally, the local Girl Scout, who sold Arianna her cookies, was astoundingly happy. She had never sold so many boxes of cookies at one house before. She told a bunch of her friends, and they all made out like bandits, taking advantage of Arianna's "Thin Mint" addiction.

Arianna felt a wave of depression wash over her. What guy would want me? She thought in despair. *No wonder Mike didn't want to marry me.*

After ten minutes of feeling sorry for herself, she pulled a muumuu-like dress, with blue and purple flowers all over it, off a hanger and paired it with white sandals, which she had bought on vacation in Hawaii, fifteen years ago. Well, this will have to do, it's the only thing that will hide my flab, she thought. *At least my toes look nice.* One of Arianna's acquaintances, Tiffany, was a "nails technician" at Meadowville's only nail salon, Carolyn's Nails. She felt sorry for Arianna after she lost her job, and had given her a few mani-pedis after- hours, on the house. To tell the truth, Tiffany enjoyed Arianna's funny stories so much, that it was worth it to her. Arianna decided to wear her hair long and bobby pin a fake purple flower over her right ear. Soon, the doorbell rang and Tony and Carmela shot like arrows under the bed. *Hmm, the cats can even sense Her Craziness approaching.* Arianna and her mother Sandra had their differences over the years. Sandra has extremely high expectations of Arianna, and she never fulfills them, was how Arianna would sum up their relationship in a nutshell.

She opened her front door and, as she expected, her mom looked at her, wrinkled her nose distastefully, and asked, "Whatever are you wearing, Arianna?"

"Didn't you know mom, the Hawaiian look is IN," she responded, while flouncing out of the house past her, leaving her mother to lock the door behind her. Sandra Archer was looking very nice, indeed. Her mother was wearing a beautiful powder blue linen dress, which accentuated her sky blue eyes and porcelain skin, and a string of small pearls around her neck. *Geez, Mom looks exactly like Sandra Dee.* The weather outside was beautiful. A glorious, cloudless spring evening, with just the trace of a cool breeze to prevent it from being too warm. She looked at her mother's red sports car, which Sandra had bought a couple of months ago, and made the sign of the cross. The car was a two-seater, it sat very low to the ground, and riding in it frightened Arianna to death. She had ridden in it twice before, and had felt like she was in a Matchbox toy car. She was certain they'd get into an accident and be crushed to death. She could easily imagine the jaws of life having to pick out her mangled body from the wreckage. That is, if they actually could lift me out with all the weight I've put on, she thought. *I am definitely going on a diet, starting now.* She didn't know what got into her mother; this car was not her style at all. Sandra was conservative and, for as long as she could remember, almost always owned a silver Buick. It was probably one of those mid-life crises she guessed, forgetting that Sandra Archer, being in her early sixties, was no longer considered "mid-life."

As soon as they both got into the vehicle, her mother started. "Now Arianna," she said, quickly glancing over at her, "these men at the dance could be potential life partners, so please behave yourself."

"Oh my God, Mom," she fumed, clenching her fists like a petulant teenager. "What do you think I'm going to do, speak in monosyllables and drool all over myself?" Her mother grimaced in response, remembering the countless times her daughter had embarrassed her in front of eligible bachelors in the past. As soon as Arianna hit her mid-twenties, her mother had been desperately trying to get her hitched. Arianna's younger sister had managed to snag an eligible bachelor, albeit in Arianna's opinion, an extremely boring one, several years ago. Emily was already married and had a little boy, Maxwell, who was cute as a button. However, Arianna strongly disliked children as a matter of principle, especially babies. She found them boring, and couldn't understand why people were so infatuated with creatures that you couldn't even hold a conversation with. Her mother was well aware of her feelings about children, but that didn't stop her from scheming to get her hitched, and dragged, kicking and screaming into motherhood. She was itching to be a grandma again, specifically, a grandmother to a little girl.

Arianna closed her eyes during most of the thankfully, short ride. Sandra constantly talked while driving, and would actually, from time to time, look over at Arianna while she was talking to her. Needless to say, her mother did not pay nearly enough close attention to the road. This resulted in Arianna having her wits scared out of her on many an occasion and becoming very stressed out. As they pulled into the parking lot, Arianna drew in a sigh of relief and practically dove out the door, almost falling, after tripping on her muumuu. She walked into the church ahead of Sandra. After her mother caught up with her in the church, Arianna was happy to see she wasn't hovering over her at all, but instead was keeping her distance. Probably embarrassed because of my outfit, she correctly guessed.

Chapter Two - The Dance

Arianna was a little nervous and didn't feel like talking to anyone right away. She headed straight towards the makeshift bar, set up off to the side, in the basement of St. Francis Church. The church was packed, like almost all other singles dances, with one man to every four women. Most of the lights were turned off and there was plenty of room to dance on a large, dark brown tiled floor. A huge red and white banner hung upon one of the cream colored walls that read, "Welcome to the St. Francis Singles Dance." There was also a disco strobe light in the corner of the room. Pink, blue and yellow lights flashed across the dance floor. *Wow, they sure go all out here, don't they?*

"Can I have a White Russian?" she asked, and then remembered her diet and changed it to a Black Russian instead. The bartender, who looked ninety if he was a day, moved like a snail, and what seemed like a lifetime later, handed her the drink. Arianna poured the vodka and coffee concoction down her throat, leaned against the bar casually and scanned the room. As expected, she was the only one wearing a Hawaiian muumuu. However, she did notice she was one of the younger and better looking attendees, even if she did, she told herself, currently look like a beached whale. She was probably the only person there who was in their thirties. There were a few in their forties, but most she'd say, were in their fifties and sixties. There were even a bunch of women, who she figured must be in their seventies, as they appeared to be caught in some 1950's time warp. These women danced "The Twist", no matter what song the DJ was playing. Most of them, she also noticed, were dressed like June Cleaver from Leave it to Beaver.

Sandra Archer was flitting to and fro, like the social butterfly that she was, resembling a gracious hostess at her dinner party. She managed to quickly visit with practically every woman there, never spending more than a couple of minutes with each one. Arianna unaccountably became annoyed. Why the heck, does she even go to these things then, if it's not to dance or meet men, she wondered. Did she come here just to chit-chat?

Most of the men seemed to be over fifty, which suited her just fine, as she preferred older men anyway. Mike, as she loved to remind him, to his chagrin, was fifty-one. She set her drink on the bar and was about to use the restroom, when an attractive man with silver hair and sparkling blue eyes walked over to her. He had a nice tan going on and was dressed very well in a blue suit, white crisp shirt, and a shiny tie with navy blue and silver diagonal stripes. She did notice he was balding a little in the back, but told herself she wouldn't hold that against him. He opened his mouth to speak, and she took the opportunity to admire his very white teeth.

Arianna's teeth, to her despair, were not white, but mildly tea and coffee stained. She had used Crest white strips in the past, but the whiteness didn't last very long, and she was too cheap to go to the dentist and get her teeth bleached. She was also too frightened. Dentists in general gave her the heebee jeebies, except for Mike's younger brother Matt, who happened to be a nice, non-sadistic dentist. Unfortunately through Arianna's HMO, she was forced to choose a dentist, who she was convinced was a sadist, much like the one in the "Little Shop of Horrors" play. The last time she went, it took four visits for her dentist to give her a root canal, subsequently causing Arianna enough significant pain and suffering, that she was forced to call in sick from work. Needless to say, she hadn't been to the dentist since then, which was over two years ago.

"I'm sorry," she said, "did you say something?"

"I was just asking you your name," the man replied, adjusting his tie.

"It's Arianna," she said, "but you can call me Riann."

"Riann," he said, "that's a pretty name for a pretty woman." She promptly blushed and asked him for his.

"Phil La Paglia."

"Oh, is that Italian?" she asked.

"Indeed, my father was Italian, Sicilian in fact, and my mother, German," he told her.

"Oh, I know an Italian, Sallie Rigelli. Do you know her?" Sallie was an acquaintance of Arianna's, who had originally asked her to look into the St. James Christian Church deaths last year.

"No, but it's not like all Italians know each other though," he chuckled.

She blushed again. "Sorry, that was a stupid question," she said, as she blew a strand of long blond hair out of her face.

"Riann, would you like to dance with me?" Phil asked, looking deep into her green eyes.

A little unnerved, she responded, "Sure, let me just get one of these appetizers here first." She had spied some mini crab cakes on a platter and inelegantly shoved one into her mouth. When she was already halfway finished eating it, she recalled her diet. "Crap," she said aloud. I need to tie a string around my finger or something, she thought.

"Excuse me?" Phil asked.

"Sorry, never mind," she replied. *Geez, I'm making a real good impression here.* He took her left hand and gently walked her onto the dance floor. "Wonderful Tonight" by Eric Clapton was playing. Phil put his right arm around her and his left hand grasped hers in the air, as he expertly led her across the dance floor.

"I love this song," she whispered.

"I do too and may I say, in spite of the chance of possibly sounding corny, that you DO look wonderful tonight."

"In this muumuu, I doubt it," Arianna replied.

Phil said, "I think you would look good wearing a burlap sack."

She blushed furiously. *Wow, this guy sure was charming.* Mike should take some lessons from him, she thought. In the past, Mike would never dance with her. He was supposedly too macho or something, to be seen dancing. One time they went to a wedding together and he refused to dance even one slow song with her, so Arianna was forced to sit out for all of them. However, when the fast songs came on, she went out on the dance floor and gave it all she got. Near the end of the night, the DJ played one of her favorite songs, "Funky Cold Medina" by Tone Loc. It just so happened, two young, attractive men loved her moves on the dance floor and made an Arianna sandwich with her in the middle.

When she finally sat down, Mike had remarked, "Jesus, Riann, why didn't you three just get a room or something?"

"You know I can't help it when that song is playing, something just takes over my body," she replied.

"Well, it was an embarrassing sight," Mike complained.

"You know, you're embarrassing, sitting here alone like a mope." She stalked off and returned to the dance floor. She had danced to Rick James', "Super Freak" and Salt n Pepa's, "Push It" (Arianna's signature song), before Mike had enough and took her home. Hmmm, if Mike could only see me now, she thought.

"Whatcha thinking about beautiful?" Phil asked.

"Oh nothing," she hastily replied. The song ended and the DJ announced, "Next up, The Black Eyed Peas with "Fergilicious"."

"Damn," she said, "they are playing some kick-ass music tonight!" Arianna noticed a lot of grumbling going on about the DJ's choice of music. Mostly everyone seemed to be appalled at the song selections, and they pretty much cleared the dance floor when the fast songs were playing. During the slow songs, she did observe; however, a few co-ed couples dancing the waltz. One very obnoxious, fat, drunk lady kept asking the DJ to play some Lawrence Welk, and was screaming, "POLKA POLKA POLKA!" at the top of her lungs. Arianna looked over at the DJ, who appeared annoyed, but managed to ignore the drunk lady, for the most part. The DJ was quite an attractive man around her age, and so, in Arianna's mind, the mystery of the contemporary song selection was laid to rest.

She mentioned this to Phil. "I'm surprised they hired such a young DJ for such an older crowd of people."

"Well," he explained, "the church was pretty desperate. The regular DJ, Ebenezer, died a week ago and the only person who could fill in on such short notice was the organist's son. Evidently, he used to DJ in college.

"Oh? What did the regular DJ die of?" she asked out of curiosity.

"Old age, I guess," said Phil.

"Old age? How old was he?" Arianna asked him.

"Well, you see Stanley over there?" He pointed at the old decrepit bartender.

"Yeah," she replied.

"He looks like an Adonis compared to Ebenezer."

"Seriously though, how old was he?"

"I really don't know, I don't think anybody really knows how old he was," Phil replied.

"But how did they manage to print up his funeral cards if nobody knew how old he was?" she asked.

"Good question," he said, "I have no idea."

"Hmmm, maybe they carbon dated him?" she theorized. "You know, like they do with fossils," she added, not understanding why Phil suddenly doubled over with laughter. *I wonder why men think everything I say is so funny?*

"Would you please dance with me?" she pleaded, remembering to bat her eyelashes. She had read somewhere that this was a fail-safe flirting technique.

"Of course I will. I'm not familiar with this song but…"

"Just follow my lead," she replied. They stayed right where they were and when the next song came on, Arianna immediately began swaying her hips and shaking her butt. To her surprise, he began imitating her perfectly, which made her laugh hysterically.

"Are you laughing at me?" Phil asked innocently, pretending to be upset.

"Yes, you look ridiculous, but cute," she added. Arianna then proceeded to show him how to "Twerk" and perform other dance moves which she knew by heart, including: the "Lawn Mower", the "Bus Driver", and always a crowd pleaser, "The Macarena." Phil was having a great time and getting quite a kick out of her.

Arianna noticed a group of three women, in their fifties or sixties, she guessed, watching the both of them and whispering. Two of the three women were blatantly glaring at the couple, which Arianna found quite disconcerting. When the dance ended and they walked off the floor together, she commented, "It appears we have an audience." She nodded in the ladies' direction.

"Indeed," he remarked, looking at the women and frowning a little. Appearing a little rattled, he defiantly slipped his arm around Arianna's waist and walked over to the side of the basement with her.

Arianna asked Phil, "Just out of curiosity, what made you decide to hit on ME specifically?"

He smiled. "Well, besides being beautiful of course, you looked like you didn't care what anyone else thought of you and you also seemed like the kind of woman who knows how to have fun."

"Wow! You must be psychic," she told him in earnest, quite amazed that he had her pegged so well. He chuckled in response. "Do you like to read?" Arianna asked.

"Sure, I love to read, and have a huge library at home," he replied.

"You do? What do you like to read most?" she eagerly asked him.

"I'd probably have to say mysteries," he answered, rubbing his chin.

"Oh my God! What kind?" Arianna had a hard time now, controlling her growing excitement.

"Well, I really love Arthur Conan Doyle's, "Sherlock Holmes" series." After hearing that, she practically ravished him. They talked for several minutes, Arianna plying him with questions about his favorite stories, his favorite quotes, which portrayal of Sherlock Holmes did he like best, etc.

"It looks like we have a lot in common," he told her. "My ex-wife is actually a big Sherlock Holmes fan as well."

"Oh? You're divorced?" Arianna said, arching one eyebrow.

"Yes, with one kid, although she's really not a kid anymore, she's thirty." He appeared suddenly somber, as if he were deep in serious thought.

"Were you married long?"

"Yes, I think so, according to most people at least, a little over twenty years."

"Wow!" she exclaimed.

He took her hand and walked over to the bar with her. "Hi Stanley, I'll have the usual please, JB and water." Phil looked over at her. "What will you have, my dear?"

She thought for a few seconds, then said, "Aww, screw it, I'll take a Kahlua and Cream on the rocks please." A couple of eons later, (that's what it felt like to Arianna at least) the elderly bartender gave them their drinks. The couple walked over and sat down to rest a while at one of the tables that the church had set up for this purpose. All of the tables were covered with nice, dark red, linen tablecloths with glowing red lanterns on them. They chatted for the next ten minutes and Arianna regaled him with tales of her annoying mother and sister.

Phil drained the last of his JB and water, and rather shakily stood up. "Will you excuse me, I'm going to go visit the men's room."

"Great idea, I need to use the restroom as well, rather badly, actually." She stood up and walked over to the bathroom. Arianna ended up peeing so much, it was ridiculous. For someone with such a small bladder, it was amazing how she could store it up like a camel, when she had to. Facing the mirror, she put more blush on and touched up her lip gloss, attempting to make her lips look as kissable as possible. She also straightened the flower in her hair, which had fallen sideways during her last dance with Phil. When she exited the bathroom, she saw him standing nearby, waiting.

He staggered towards her and said, "I don't feel well."

Arianna, noticing his face was flushed and his pupils were dilated, worriedly asked, "Oh my gosh, what's wrong?" as they began to walk back across the dance floor.

"I dunno, I justs feels odd," Phil said, slurring his speech. "Ohmy Lerd, there id is!" he suddenly cried out, pointing towards the wall.

"There what is?" she asked in a concerned voice.

"De spazeship of course, doncha see it?" he urgently replied.

"What are you talking about?" she said, now frightened.

He looked at Arianna and suddenly his eyes widened, "OhmaGod, ohmaGod, they're allz over you!" he slurred.

"What's all over me?" she asked, confused.

"De spiderz!" he yelled.

"Whaaa?" Arianna frantically inspected her muumuu. Phil suddenly slumped to the floor in a convulsive fit.

"Oh Jesus Christ, someone please help him!" she cried out hysterically. People started rushing towards them from everywhere. The music had stopped and the lights were turned back on.

Arianna's mother came over and yelled in a frantic voice, "Arianna, what did you do to him??"

"Nothing! I swear I didn't do anything, Mom. He started saying weird things, and then just collapsed and started convulsing," she answered, sounding extremely worried.

The DJ, a tall, muscular, blond, blue-eyed man in his mid-to-late thirties, swiftly came over and said, "I'm a doctor, please let me through." *Hmmm, he's attractive, has great taste in music, and he's a doctor... Potential hubby perhaps?* Okay, wait a minute Arianna, focus, she told herself. Phil is unconscious and he needs help. By this time, he had stopped convulsing. The DJ rested two fingers against the side of Phil's neck, looked up and informed her, "I'm afraid he's dead."

"What?" Arianna felt she must not have heard him correctly.

"I'm afraid he's dead, no pulse, no heartbeat." Arianna stood there in shock, her eyes glistening with tears. Everyone gasped and started whispering amongst themselves.

Arianna overheard one of the ladies who had been watching the two of them, a short chubby woman with auburn hair, remark rather loudly, "He probably had a heart attack from dancing crazy with that floozy."

To her surprise, before she could even respond, her mother defended her. "My daughter is NOT a floozy, and we demand an apology!" she ordered, standing tall with both hands on her hips. The woman appearing contrite, mumbled something and then quickly walked away with the other women.

"Hey, thanks Mom," Arianna whispered.

"Nobody insults one of my daughters and gets away with it," Sandra Archer declared and walked briskly away.

Arianna tapped the DJ, who was still kneeling over Phil's body, on the shoulder. "Umm, excuse me, what's your name?"

He looked up at her and replied, "Frank."

"Frank, do you think it was some sort of epileptic seizure?" she asked. "He was acting very strangely right before he collapsed."

"How so?" Frank asked, suddenly focusing his attention on her.

"Well, among other things, he was staggering and complained he didn't feel well. He was also talking about seeing spaceships on the wall, and he said that there were spiders all over me," she replied. "Are these symptoms of epilepsy?"

A woman who was standing nearby, with a blond beehive hairdo and cat-eye glasses, interrupted their conversation. "Hello, I'm Sarah Brewster and I'm in charge of these dances. I've known Phil for years and he was not an epileptic."

"Well, off the top of my head," Frank said grimly, "it appears he could have taken some hallucinogenic drug." Right then, they could hear the ambulance sirens outside. Someone must have called 911 rather quickly, Arianna thought.

"That is preposterous, Phil would never do such a thing!" Sarah replied adamantly. This was Arianna's worst nightmare, almost like an Agatha Christie novel. Suddenly, she heard heavy footsteps behind her and her nightmare got even worse.

"What exactly happened here?" Arianna slowly turned around to see Mike standing there, looking quite serious. Mike Stevenson was six feet tall, well-built, and even though he was over fifty and balding, he could be quite intimidating, with his piercing blue eyes, grey beard and mustache.

Arianna sighed deeply. "This man," she said, pointing at the body, "Phil La Paglia, suddenly collapsed and died while having some sort of fit or seizure." She walked over and sat down at one of the tables closest to the body.

Frank stood up and shook hands with Mike. "I'm Dr. Frank Murphy and right now I'm thinking this might have been an LSD or PCP overdose," he told him.

"Oh?" Mike knelt down by the body and avoided looking at Arianna.

"Do you think it was rabies?" she asked the doctor.

"Rabies, what makes you think it was rabies?"

"A couple of the symptoms of rabies are delusions and convulsions. I learned this a few weeks ago, from an episode of Criminal Minds," Arianna explained. "This was, of course, before I stopped watching the series," she added.

"Well, there's no foaming at the mouth, so no, I don't believe it was rabies," Frank replied, giving her a funny look.

Mike stood up and in a very loud voice shouted, "Attention, attention, nobody leaves here until either, Sergeant Tennyson, Sergeant Barelli, or myself, takes your statements and gives the okay to release you, understood?" Looking shocked and dismayed, everyone slowly nodded.

"Good, it's going to be a long night!"

Despite loving the fact that her mother was going to be questioned by the police, Arianna felt very depressed. She imagined that Phil could've been a contender, and she didn't even get around to asking him yet, what he did for a living. She was tired, her feet hurt, and she very much wanted to go home. About twenty minutes later, she got up and walked over to Mike, who had just finished taking down some woman's statement. "Hey, I really need to get home OK, so can you please let me go?" she whined.

"No can do, you're not going anywhere," he informed her.

"But, but I just remembered, I forgot to give Tony and Carmela their water."

"So?"

"They both have medical issues, they could die of thirst," she lied.

"Riann, we need a statement from you first. Actually, your statement will probably be the most helpful of all, so...sit...down," he sounded the words out slowly. She knew better than to continue to argue with Mike when he got that look on his face.

"So be it, let their slow agonizing deaths be on your head," she said dramatically, hiked up her muumuu, and sat back down.

Fifteen minutes later, she noticed Mike and her mother laughing, and acting all buddy-buddy with each other. Sandra even had her hand on his back. Arianna looked at them both suspiciously.

"Alright, have a good evening Michael," her mother told him and started to leave.

Arianna perked up, "Oh, we can leave now?"

"Sandra can go, but you still need to be interviewed."

"What?" Arianna yelled, clearly upset. Her mother waved goodbye. "Goodnight, dear," she called out to her, quickly exiting the church.

"That was my ride you know, we came together," Arianna whined.

"Don't worry, I'm driving you home," Mike reassured her.

She gave him a dirty look. "I'd rather walk."

"Really, with your 'exercise-induced asthma' that comes on after walking a block or two?" She folded her arms across her chest and silently glared at him. "Wow, if looks could kill," he remarked. She still said nothing. "Riann, if you want to get out of here soon, you'll have to answer some questions."

"Alright, ask away," she said snottily.

"Tell me what happened tonight," he said. "Oh, and just stick to anything that might be relevant."

Arianna looked offended. "Well, first I was trying to decide what to wear and, unfortunately, nothing in my closet fit, to my amazement, except for this muumuu…"

"Stop, I don't need to know all that, just start from when you first entered the church," he impatiently interrupted. He spoke to her as if she was a child, "Remember, stick only to things that might be relevant."

"Geez, I'm just trying to give you a clear picture of the night as it unfolded. Anyway, my mother went off on her own, thank God, and I went to the bar. That ancient man over there," she said, pointing to Stanley the bartender, "poured me a Black Russian, which took forever. I walked around and Phil, overtaken in rapture by my loveliness, approached me and introduced himself," she paused, as Mike was rolling his eyes and finding it difficult not to interrupt her again, "and then we talked."

"Did he look alright? Did he mention not feeling well?" he pressed her.

"No, it wasn't until later that he said he didn't feel right," she replied. "He did tell me he was divorced and had a grown daughter. That was about it, he was mostly asking me questions about myself."

Mike prodded her, "Then, what happened?"

"He asked me to dance, that's what happened. Unlike SOME people, he actually enjoyed dancing. It was so refreshing to have a male dance partner, not so insecure that he can't..."

"Riann, cut it!" Mike said, tapping his right foot impatiently.

"Fine," she replied resentfully. "We danced to "Wonderful Tonight" and then to "Fergilicious"."

"Yes, I've heard you made quite the spectacle of yourself," he said.

"Oh, those old prunes can kiss my ass," she retorted.

Mike sighed and asked, "What happened, then?"

"We went to the bar and the old coot gave him his JB and water and me a Kahlua and Cream, which Phil paid for, of course," she added, looking at him smugly. "We sat down at that table," she pointed to a table near the DJ, "and talked for about ten minutes or so and finished our drinks. I was delighted to hear, that Phil was quite the avid reader, and like myself, very much appreciated Sir Arthur Conan Doyle's...," her voice trailed off, when she noticed Mike glaring at her again. "Umm, then we decided to use the restrooms."

"How did he look at this point?" Mike questioned her.

"He seemed a little shaky, I guess," she replied. "I just figured I had exhausted him with my hot sexy dance moves," she said, wiggling her hips. Mike sighed deeply. "Afterwards, we met each other outside the bathrooms, and he kind of staggered towards me and said he didn't feel well. He was all flushed and his pupils were dilated. I asked him what was wrong while we were walking across the dance floor to find an empty table. He said he didn't know and was slurring his words. Then, all of a sudden, he pointed to the wall and said he saw a spaceship there and asked me if I saw it. After that, he began screaming that I had spiders all over me, which freaked me out big time, because you know how I feel about spiders." Mike did know, because he, unfortunately, had happened to be around Arianna on many occasions when she spotted a millipede or spider. She would scream bloody murder and jump on whatever was closest to her, whether it be a chair, a sofa, or Mike himself. You would have thought she had a saber-toothed tiger in her home, and not just an itty bitty spider, he often thought to himself. Arianna continued, "Then, he collapsed, started having convulsions, and well, died." Arianna's lower lip started trembling.

Mike said, "Wait here." A couple of minutes later, he returned and said, "Okay, it looks like Phil has officially been pronounced dead by the medical examiner. We can leave now."

"Oh thank God, so what did he die of?" she asked.

"We don't know yet, we have to wait for the toxicology report, which we won't get for a couple of days," he replied.

"Hey," she suddenly perked up, "this is like the perfect time for you guys to use me as a consultant on this case."

"A consultant for what?" he asked, sounding confused.

"To find out who killed him, of course."

"Killed him? What makes you automatically jump to the conclusion that he was killed?" Mike asked.

"That Sarah woman said Phil was not epileptic and we know he was clearly hallucinating."

"Yeah, so?"

"You heard what Frank said, it could have been some hallucinogenic drug," she explained.

"So what if it was, it wouldn't be the first time some bozo overdosed on some drug," Mike told her.

"Phil was not a bozo and definitely not the type to willingly take a hallucinogenic drug," Arianna said adamantly.

"How would you know? You knew him for what, all of forty-five minutes?"

"I just know, that's all," she replied with a stubborn look on her face.

"I think you're biased," he told her.

"And I think you're jealous because I was having a good time with another man."

"No, that's ridiculous. Give me a little more credit than that. I don't let my personal life interfere with my professional life," Mike stated.

"Well, I have a gut feeling his death was NOT due to natural causes, NOR was it accidental. If you don't let me consult on this Mike, I will nag you for the rest of your life," she threatened him.

"That's a risk I'm willing to take," Mike replied. "Don't you think you're making a mountain out of a molehill, because you're bored and want to solve a mystery?"

"Whatever, can we just go? I'm tired," Arianna pleaded.

"I suppose so. Listen, if it makes you happy, after we get the results back from the lab, if there's anything suspicious, I'll tell my boss, Ed, the Police Superintendent about your offer, OK?" Arianna folded her arms across her chest but said nothing, all of a sudden feeling exhausted.

Mike drove her home, enduring the uncomfortable silence which pervaded the entire ride. When he reached Arianna's house, he barely had time to come to a full stop, when she jumped out of the car. Unfortunately, her muumuu got stuck in the car door and whipped her body back. Blushing, she said, "Kindly release my muumuu, I mean dress, from your car door." Mike, trying to contain a smile, opened the door for her. She pulled her dress back, stalked up to her front door and let herself in for the night.

Chapter Three - Arlene

The next morning, Arianna woke up very sad. *Geez, the first time I meet a decent guy in a long time, and he up and croaks on me.* She stumbled out of bed wearing an old over-sized, navy blue "Meadowville P.D." t-shirt, which Mike gave her a few years ago, and walked into the kitchen. She opened the refrigerator door and grabbed herself some apple juice. As she was pouring herself a glass, she replayed last night's events in her mind. *I knew going anywhere with my mother could only lead to trouble, I should have known better. Maybe, I should try LustMatch. I think Sallie Rigelli told me she had a lot of luck with that. Of course, Sallie would also have luck dialing random numbers from the phone book.* Arianna's cell phone, on the kitchen counter, started vibrating. She looked down at it, her sister Emily was calling.

"Hey what's up?" Arianna asked, leaning her back against the counter.

"Riann, are you okay? Mom told me what happened last night."

"Oh, yeah, what a debacle, but I'm fine," she replied, sighing. She pulled out one of the tall bar stools that were lined up against her kitchen counter and took a seat.

"Mom said you were all hot and heavy with some old geezer," said Emily.

"You know, I'm gonna kill Mom, she's so freakin annoying. There's not much to tell, I'm sorry to say. This guy Phil and I had danced a few dances together, and then he hallucinated, had a fit, and dropped dead. That's it, end of story," Arianna recounted, sounding exasperated.

"OK, OK, I believe you. She also said the cops questioned you guys. What do you think happened?" she asked.

"I don't know, I guess he might have taken or was slipped some hallucinogenic drug," Arianna replied.

"Really, like what?"

"I don't know. Listen Emily, I'm not really in a mood to talk right now; I'm a little depressed. I thought there was a good chance of meeting somebody there, and then this happens. I'm even contemplating trying LustMatch out."

"LustMatch? That sounds sleazy. Why don't you let Bill and I set you up?" Bill was Emily's nice, dependable husband, who drove Arianna crazy with his long, pointless, boring stories, which only he found hilarious.

"Set me up? Ohhh, I don't know," she replied, sounding wary.

"C'mon Riann, Bill says there are lots of single guys where he works."

"Yeah, but Bill doesn't know what type of guy I like," Arianna explained.

"Well, why don't you give me an idea of what you want in a man, and I'll write it down and give it to him," Emily suggested.

"Alright, well first, he's got to be tall, that's EXTREMELY important."

"OK, tall, anything else?" Emily asked, while jotting that down on a pad of paper she kept next to the phone.

"He can't be super fat or excessively thin. He has to be average weight, or slightly under or slightly over. He would preferably not wear glasses, but that's not a deal breaker. A beard would be awesome too. He must be outgoing, but not obnoxious. He has to be funny, but not funnier than me. He must watch lots of TV, and oh, I almost forgot, he must like to read. Especially mysteries, not the gory, bloody, serial killer kind, but the cozy mystery genre like Agatha Christie. You know death in a small village, that sort of thing." She paused for a second.

"Oh, and he must be of Nordic, Germanic or British descent and fair complected. Blond, light brown, grey or silver hair. No baldies! Eyes that are preferably blue, green, or hazel, but that's not mandatory. He's got to be affectionate, but not clingy. Must be a non-smoker. Has to be very smart, but not too smart. Like, not arrogant, you know? Well, maybe a little arrogant. He should have at least a Bachelor's degree, but not in anything boring. Of course, anything in the Humanities would be ideal."

Emily, who had stopped writing after "he must like to read", sighed, "Well, this would explain why you're still single. Are you finished?"

"No, I..."

"You're finished," Emily said. "We'll see what we can do. SERIOUSLY though Riann, you're being ridiculous."

"Well excuse me, you're the one who asked," replied Arianna, mildly affronted. "But thanks Em, I do appreciate your efforts."

"*Adios,*" said her sister, as she closed the phone.

Arianna looked at the clock. Oh wow, I need to get ready for work, she reminded herself. She pulled her soft pink and baby blue waitress uniform off the hanger in her closet. Because she worked at Sandy's Diner, a recreation of the years when rock n roll reigned, the waitress uniforms were straight out of the 1950's. It could be worse, she thought, I could have "Arianna" written in cursive over my left breast. She twisted her hair up into a bun and pinned it with a black hair clip. She pulled on her last pair of run-free pantyhose and slipped on her shoes. Then she put bright red lipstick and heavy black mascara on, petted both of her cats and left her house. She ran over to her eleven year-old, red Chevy Cavalier and drove about ten minutes until she reached the restaurant.

"Late again?" Pete, Arianna's short, bald, and pudgy boss, greeted her at the door. True to its 50's theme, Sandy's Diner had a few really nice jukeboxes, a menu full of soda fountain favorites, as well as traditional meals, and a bunch of salty waitresses. Although, of course, every time she was salty, she got in trouble, Arianna thought resentfully.

She looked at her watch. "Seriously Pete, one lousy minute?" He shook his head at her and walked away. Arianna was actually the youngest waitress there and so all the older waitresses gave her a rough time. They were hard and bitter chain-smokers, who worked there for years and didn't take kindly to the young newbie. They complained to Pete about everything Arianna did and she always ended up with the worst station. They told her the station schedule went by seniority, and so basically, the only way she could move up Arianna figured, was if one of the old bats kicked the bucket. Judging by how much most of them smoked, she thought they were extremely lucky to still be alive.

She punched her card in the time clock and went to her station, which, as usual, consisted of a paltry three tables. She swore that Pete purposely gave her the customers that tipped the least: old ladies, women with small children, and teenagers, in that order. Middle-aged businessmen who smoked were the best tippers, but unfortunately, she never seemed to get them at her tables. She looked around and was pleased to see that there were no teenagers sitting in her station at the moment. Teenagers annoyed her immensely because they never ordered a normal meal, only a bunch of side dishes. They also, for some inexplicable reason, laughed at everything Arianna said. She truly believed all teenagers were high and just came in there because they had the munchies. This would explain their cheapness she figured, because they probably spent all their cash on weed. A typical order for a teenager went something like this:

Arianna: "Can I take your order please?"

Teen boy: "Ha, ha, ha, I'll have a, ha, ha, ha chocolate shake, a side of fries, a side of onion rings, ha ha ha ha ha and a side of mozzarella sticks, ha ha ha ha ha!!!"

Arianna did not believe in making small talk with her customers at all, so that was one variable that might have had an impact on her tips. She refused on principle, to suck up to her customers and pretend like she actually gave a crap about their lives. She felt she had enough problems to deal with. Her opinion was, in a nutshell, that the customers were there to eat; therefore, she'd take their order promptly, deliver their food quickly, stay close in case she was needed, and then hand them their check as soon as possible. She'd often ask Mike, "What's wrong with that? That's what I'd want in a waitress." Mike tried to tell her that a lot of people liked to talk to their waitress. He attempted to explain to her that talking to waitresses helped break up the monotony of their mundane lives. "Then they should just get a cat," reasoned Arianna. "If I need to talk, Tony and Carmela are always available." Mike would just roll his eyes. However, he knew what those cats meant to her, so at that point he'd usually just change the subject.

The lunch rush was coming in, which meant she got stuck with a group of regulars, old ladies who always complained everything was too salty and that the restaurant was freezing. Arianna, who 99% of the time was sweating bullets, did what she always does when they complain, lie and tell them she'll be sure to tell the boss. Another reason why Arianna disliked waiting on them so much, was that she was forced to constantly repeat herself, which she found extremely frustrating. She willed herself to walk over to their table, took her pen out from behind her right ear, and attempted to take their order.

The first old lady, dressed in layers of ivory-white sweaters, asked, "Can you tell me please, what are your soups of the day?"

"Split pea and beef noodle," Arianna said.

"Oh, I'll have a bowl of split pea." Arianna wrote it down on her check pad.

The second old lady, making quite a show of shivering, asked, "Excuse me, what are your salad dressings?"

"French, Italian, garlic, and our house dressing," she replied in a robotic monotone.

"I'll have a tossed salad with garlic dressing," she decided.

Arianna looked pointedly at the third old lady. The third old lady told her, "I'll have a cup of soup."

Arianna asked, "Which kind?"

"Oh," she paused, "what kind do you have?"

Arianna groaned and replied, "Split pea and beef noodle."

"Oh, in that case, I'll have beef noodle."

"I'll take a salad," the fourth old lady told her.

Arianna asked, "What kind of dressing?"

She wrinkled her brow and said, "Oh, I'm sorry, what do you have?"

Arianna sighed deeply, feeling like she would actually welcome death at that moment. Of course when they were all gone, she was left with a pitiful tip, for each one of them had dumped a pile of small change next to their coffee cup.

Another table she got stuck with was a harried looking woman with three kids; a five year-old and two year-old twins. Luckily, it was springtime, and so she didn't have to deal with the mother taking forever to undress the children from layers upon layers of cumbersome winter clothing. However, getting the high chairs and booster seat set up took quite a while and tested Arianna's patience. Waiting on people with kids effectively ruined Arianna's usual waitressing mantra of, "in and out, in and out". After everyone was situated, the toddlers began playing with all the breadsticks and crackers from the bread basket. They alternately crumbled them up all over the floor, or shoved them into their mouths and then spat everything out on the table. The five year-old threw every single jelly and sugar packet on the floor, and then opened and drank each one of the creamers. What was wrong with this woman? Arianna thought. Why didn't she just stop at having one? Next, to her chagrin, the mother insisted on having her five year-old son order for himself.

"May I take your order?" asked Arianna.

The mother in a whiny baby voice said, "Tell the nice waitress what you want, Micky."

"Wah!" cried Micky.

Arianna, impatiently shifting from one foot to the other, looked at the kid and said, "Yes?"

"Wah! I want peanut butter!"

"No honey, they don't have peanut butter here. How about a nice grilled cheese instead?" suggested the mother.

"No! Wah!" he responded.

"Well, how about a hot dog then?"

"No, no, no, I don't want a hot dog, wah!"

Despite having to put up with all that, Arianna ended up receiving a cheap tip. She wasn't surprised at all. Giving decent tips were evidently not a high priority to young mothers. By the time she left the restaurant, the mother was cranky, irritable, and apparently, in a less than generous mood. Arianna was miffed that, as usual, she had to deal with all of that aggravation, and was left with nothing to show for it, but a big giant headache. Thank goodness, she only had to work until 2:30, she couldn't wait to get home.

About an hour after she arrived home, Arianna's doorbell rang. She looked through her peephole, yanked open the door and sullenly remarked, "Oh, it's you." She turned away from Mike and walked back inside. He followed closely behind her, after shutting and locking the door first. As she turned around to face him, she sarcastically commented, "Well, to what do I owe this pleasure?" She threw herself down on her couch and refused to look at him.

"Riann, the lab results are in on Phil La Paglia. I turned in a favor at the medical examiner's office and received the results back early. Phil was tested for LSD, PCP, Psilocybin, Ketamine, DXM, and Salvia Divinorum, and he came up clean for all of them."

She sat upright, suddenly interested and alert. "I don't even know what half of those are," she replied, wrinkling her brow.

"He also came up clean for the common poisons: arsenic, cyanide and strychnine. The contents of Phil's stomach revealed only lamb, a little red wine and scotch. He also seemed to be in perfect health, which was verified by his own personal doctor. What that means is his death is a mystery," Mike added, sighing. He looked over at her sheepishly. "Actually Ed, my boss, told me to stop fooling around and listen to you. He wants Phil's death investigated to make certain nothing criminal occurred."

"Oh?" Arianna grinned. "Very interesting. So, is the high and mighty Mike Stevenson here to eat crow or what?"

"Evidently, Ed was quite impressed with your work on the St. James' murders, and since you happened to be at the scene of the crime for this one, I'm supposed to formally ask you to be a paid consultant for the Meadowville Police Department on this case."

"Hmmm, really? Well, I'll have to think about that for a while. I do have a lot going on right...," Arianna replied.

"Riann..." Mike was losing his patience and his face was turning redder and redder.

"Oh, all right, if you need me that badly, then I guess I will."

"Good, I'll fill you in on everything," he said, sitting down at her dining room table on one of her high-backed, floral upholstered chairs, long used as scratching posts by Tony and Carmela.

"Just let me make one phone call first," she said, pulling out her cell phone and quickly tapping in a number. "Yeah, can I speak to Peter please?" A minute passed while she waited for him to pick up the phone. "Hi Pete, I'm going to have to hand in my notice. How much notice? Ummm, about sixteen hours notice," she answered, looking at her dining room clock. Before she hung up, Mike could hear loud shouting coming from the other end of the line.

"Boy, remind me to never again pull any strings and get you a job. You're burning all the bridges I've managed to build all these years," he complained.

"Oh, Pete's an ass, why do you think he's always short on waitresses?" she said, waving her hand dismissively.

"Right, anyway, let's get down to business. Phil's parents are deceased and he was an only child. We found out Phil's next of kin is his daughter Paula, who is thirty and single. He also has an ex-wife, Arlene, who lives in Somerset Hills. I thought we'd go visit Arlene today and talk to her."

"Fine by me, let me get changed," she replied. She slipped on simple black slacks, black dress shoes, and a navy blue, buttoned down shirt, which closely resembled the standard Meadowville police uniform. She also had her hair up and didn't wear any makeup at all because she wanted to appear as tough and masculine looking as possible. Arianna quickly grabbed a notebook and pen from her desk drawer, and shortly thereafter, they both left her house and climbed into Mike's police car.

Mike looked at her. "You know Riann, we hired you as a consultant, not a cop."

"I know that!" she replied, sounding insulted.

"Then why are you dressed as my "Mini-Me"?"

She made an "hmmph" noise in response to his question. It was warm and extremely sunny out, so she pulled her sunglasses out of her purse. Her sister Emily called them her "Jackie O" glasses, as they had big black frames, which resembled the pair Jackie was often seen wearing after her marriage to Aristotle Onassis. Arianna didn't care, she thought they were quite fashionable. She rolled down her window, stuck her right arm out, reached downward, and began drumming the outside of the car door with her fingertips. She thought it was pretty cool to be riding along with Mike in the front seat, like she was his partner. Arianna hoped people she knew would be outdoors and notice them together in the police car. She was attempting to appear as tough as possible, trying to resemble a serious cop, hot on the trail of a perp. They drove in silence for the next minute or so until they reached a red light and he turned to look at her.

"Hey," he said, sounding concerned, "are you constipated or something?"

"Nooo," she answered, frowning at him.

"Then why do you have that constipated look on your face?"

"Never mind," Arianna replied, in an annoyed tone of voice. "So, what do we know about Phil's wife?"

"Arlene's been divorced from Phil for about ten years and she's an ex-model. One of my men, who notified her of her ex-husband's death, said she's a real looker."

"Well, of course, obviously Phil knew great beauty when he saw it," she said smugly.

About ten minutes later, they entered the town of Somerset Hills. Somerset Hills was an upper middle-class suburb outside of Chicago, which consisted of some nice old Victorians, as well as big sprawling estates. Soon, they reached a very long, twisted driveway that led to Arlene La Paglia's home. Her house resembled an English country estate, complete with creeping ivy on the walls. Arianna couldn't help but ooh and ahh over it as they exited the police car and walked to the front door.

"I had no idea Phil's family was so rich." She sighed. "Boy, I really missed out on my meal ticket."

"Now get a grip Riann. Remember, we're investigating a possible murder here and she's a suspect."

"Seriously Mike? I AM a professional, I already have two solved murders under my belt, you know." They had walked up to a beautiful ornate wooden door, which featured a huge lion's head door knocker, in addition to a standard doorbell.

Arianna couldn't resist playing with the knocker. She knocked once, then twice, and then to Mike's chagrin, began knocking to the tune of Black Sabbath's, "Iron Man." "Really, Riann?" Mike frowned and clamped his hand down over hers. At that moment, the door opened to reveal a man dressed in a complete formal butler's uniform. If he was annoyed by Arianna's knocking, he didn't show it.

"Hello, may I help you?" he asked in a very dignified manner.

"Yes, this is Arianna Archer." Mike pointed at her. "She's a consultant for the Meadowville Police Department." Hmmm, I like the sound of that, Arianna thought. "And I'm Mike Stevenson, Chief of the Meadowville Police. We'd like to take a few minutes of Arlene La Paglia's time."

"I will see if Madame is receiving any visitors, please wait here." He bowed and walked away.

"'See if Madame is receiving any visitors?' Wow, he stepped right out of an Agatha Christie novel," she exclaimed.

"Well, I hate to tell Jeeves this, but Madame has no choice but to receive THESE two visitors," Mike replied in a loud voice.

"Shh, he'll hear you," Arianna whispered. "Geez, I feel seriously underdressed now. I should have worn makeup at least. Do I look bad or do I just look like a cop?"

"Don't worry about it," he told her, "you just look like a lesbian cop, that's all." She gave him a dirty look.

A few moments later, the butler returned. "Please step into the drawing room and make yourself comfortable." He led them both into a large room with ivory-colored marble floors, and thick, burgundy colored, velvet drapes on each of the six large windows in the room, held back by enormous gold ties with tassels. There was a huge mahogany chess set sitting in front of a giant fireplace. In one corner sat an enormous globe about four feet in diameter. All of it was simply breathtaking. They both took a seat on a burgundy-colored couch, which Arianna believed, was the softest, most comfortable couch she had ever sat on.

"Coffee or tea?" the butler offered.

"No thank you," Mike replied, taking his hat off and leaning forward on the sofa.

"Tea please," Arianna responded eagerly.

"It would be my pleasure Miss." He bowed, and backing out of the room, closed the double doors in front of him.

"Oh my God!" Arianna exclaimed, "this is just like <u>Downton Abbey</u>!" They sat in silence for a few minutes until the butler returned, arriving through a small entranceway in the back right-hand corner of the room. He was carrying an enormous silver tea tray, complete with pitchers, bowls, and cups and a platter of assorted cookies and cakes.

"Would you like milk or cream, Miss?" he asked.

"Oh, cream please."

"Lemon?" he asked.

"No, thank you," she answered.

"Sugar?"

"Yes," replied Arianna eagerly.

"One lump or two?"

"Two will be fine, thank you."

He walked over to a small table and brought out and opened a big brown case in front of her, revealing several rows of different types of tea; including, Earl Grey, Orange Pekoe, Chamomile, and Oolong.

"Earl Grey would be delightful," she answered slightly stunned, and made her selection. *Wow, I could really get used to this type of living.*

The butler nodded and closed the case, setting it on the table. "Madame will be with you momentarily." He then backed out of the room, closing the huge ornate doors in front of him, but not before he bowed once to her.

"Delightful?" Mike asked, turning to look at her.

"Oh shut up," she said, as she took a big bite out of a delicious macaroon.

A minute or two later, a tall, slender but shapely, beautiful woman of around fifty-five years of age, walked into the room. She had shoulder-length dishwater blonde hair, mixed with streaks of auburn, and deep blue eyes. Her nails were painted gold and looked immaculate. Hmm, she thought, after staring down at her badly chipped and chewed upon nails, I should ask Arlene who does her nails; Tiffany hasn't been up to par lately. Arianna wished she could sit on her hands during this interview.

"Hello, what can I help you two with today?" she asked them.

Mike began, "We'd just like to ask you a few questions about your ex-husband." Arianna uncapped her pen and got ready to take notes.

"I thought that was probably why you were here. I'm still somewhat in shock over the whole thing. Phil was always very healthy, very active, and in great condition."

"Ms. La Paglia…," he started to say.

"Please," she interrupted, "call me Arlene."

"Very well. Arlene, do you know of anyone who might have wanted to harm your ex-husband?"

"No, no, why?" she said, sounding alarmed.

Mike reassured her, "Just some questions we need to get out of the way ma'am."

"But you wouldn't be asking that, if he had died of natural causes," she said.

"We don't know how he died yet ma'am, would you mind answering the question," he asked. Arianna shot him an annoyed, how dare you look.

"Of course." She thought for a few seconds and then answered, "No, I honestly don't. I think Phil had always been well-liked and respected by everyone." She stared at the wall behind them and began reminiscing. "You know, Phil and I had quite an amicable divorce. He was a nice and decent man, but I really felt I needed to find myself, I guess. I realized I couldn't do that tied down, so I initiated the separation. I know this makes me sound horrible, but my daughter Paula was grown and I didn't want to be anyone's wife and mother anymore. I just wanted to be my own person, if that makes any sense.

Before we met, I had done very well for myself as a runway model in New York. Phil was on a business trip there and I was late for a photo shoot. We literally ran into each other on the street. Pretty hard, as I recall. His papers went flying, for it was an exceptionally windy day. We both apologized profusely, and he gave me his business card. He told me he was going to be there for eight days and would love to make it up to me with dinner sometime. 'Sometime' turned out to be the very next evening. We discovered that there was a tremendous mutual physical attraction between us. Phil is, was, I guess I should say," she corrected herself, "a very handsome man."

"Well, it's obvious Phil clearly had very fine taste in women," Arianna replied. Arlene, who blushed in response, wasn't sure after taking note of Arianna's attire, if this was her subtle way of making a pass at her. Arianna looked at Mike out of the corner of her eye. He frowned back at her as if to say, "knock it off".

"And that was it, we fell in love." Arlene smiled, lost in a pleasant memory.

"What type of business was Phil in?" Mike asked.

"He was an interior designer, mainly designing top-of-the-line unique pieces of furniture for the Gold Coast set. He was very good at what he did and rose up the ranks pretty quickly at the company where he worked." Arlene's eyes started to fill up, but she managed to compose herself nicely.

"Arlene, are you familiar with St. Francis Christian Church?"

"Of course, Phil and I were married there and Paula was baptized there. I can't speak for Phil, but my daughter and I still attend a handful of services a year. I do remember seeing him there on a couple of special occasions, like Christmas and Easter. As you know, he did attend the Singles Dances," Arlene replied.

"So Phil was retired, is that right?" Arlene nodded in response. "Was he currently conducting business with anyone?" he asked her.

"Not that I know of," she replied.

"How about close friends, girlfriends, did he have any?"

"As far as I know, no. Phil was a private man, mostly consumed with his work. He never really had any close male friends. He always felt most comfortable in the company of females. That didn't make him a ladies man or anything, because he truly liked women, and he was a gentleman to the core. He found them quite interesting, and physically attractive, of course," she answered, smiling.

"Thank you." Mike stood up and Arianna did the same, putting her notebook and pen back in her purse. "You've been very helpful. One last thing, can you tell me where you were in the late afternoon and evening of your ex-husband's death?" Arianna groaned and shot him a dirty look.

"Certainly, in the late afternoon I was fixing a big roast for dinner. In the evening, I was curled up in my bedroom with my cocker spaniel, Watson, watching <u>Sherlock</u> on the BBC."

"Oh my God!" Arianna exclaimed, clapping her hands together. "I LOVE <u>Sherlock</u>! Aren't Benedict Cumberbatch and Martin Freeman the best actors you've ever seen? And isn't the writing just spectacular...," her voice trailed off, as she noticed Mike glaring at her.

"I totally agree with you Arianna," Arlene said, smiling.

"Oh, please call me Riann, and by the way, I love your house and your butler too."

"Well, thank you Riann, and feel free to stop by anytime and I'll give you a tour. I'll even show you a few pieces of furniture that Phil designed himself."

"I would love that," she replied enthusiastically.

Mike interrupted, what he judged as their idle chatter, "Can anyone else verify that you were home Arlene?"

"I live alone, but my housekeeper Claudette was here. We ate dinner together and then she stayed for awhile finishing up laundry. I don't know when she actually left though, but I did speak to her a couple of times."

"Thank you, have a good day." He clasped Arianna's arm and walked out the door before she could say anything.

"Ow, you're hurting me!" she yelled, when they reached his car.

"Riann, you cannot act like that when we're in the middle of questioning a suspect," he told her.

"Oh why not, for Pete's sake?" she replied, annoyed. "It's clear to me she's not a killer."

"Oh yeah, and how exactly do you know that?"

"Look how kind and gracious and pretty she is and just look at her beautiful home…"

Mike cut her off, "Oh my God, seriously Riann? You think only mean, ugly people are killers?"

Arianna blushed. "No, of course not. On the TV show Elementary, they adapted the character of Sherlock Holmes' nemesis, Professor James Moriarty and made him a woman. 'Jamie Moriarty' was a wealthy and beautiful woman, but also a dangerous killer," she replied, "anyway, I like her."

"Alright, we need to maintain an impartial, professional attitude at all times, got it?" said Mike.

"Yes Sir!" she rolled her eyes and saluted him.

He looked down at his phone. "Listen, I just got a reply to a text I sent inquiring about the state of Arlene's finances. It turns out she had most of her money in the stock market, and with the recent recession, she took a very deep hit." He looked up and added, "I wouldn't be surprised if she started selling off her assets soon."

Arianna said, "Well, that certainly isn't good. Oh, can you please check out Arlene's story about her divorce being amicable? I want to make sure she was telling us the truth about that."

"Will do," Mike promised.

"One more thing, I couldn't get a word in edgewise there. Can I be the one who questions the daughter?"

"Fine. Again, just remember, remain detached and objective. Any of these people could potentially be a killer."

Arianna grunted, then declared, "Nobody who has taste that great could possibly be a murderer, except for Professor Moriarty, of course."

"Riann, this isn't a book or TV," he warned. "Why don't we go visit Paula now, then later I'll go back to the station and have one of my guys verify Arlene's alibi with her housekeeper?"

"Sure, but I still don't understand why we're even questioning Arlene and Paula. We know they weren't at the dance."

"Yeah, but since we don't know exactly how he was drugged, I just want to make sure neither woman was with him just prior to the dance," Mike explained.

"Okey Dokey," she replied, cracking her knuckles and looking forward to the next interview.

Chapter Four - Paula

The couple buckled their seat belts, and before they knew it, they were back in Meadowville. Mike parked in front of a modest bungalow with a small front yard filled with weeds and grass, which desperately needed to be cut. The pair walked up to the door, knocked twice, and then rang the bell. Because no one answered, they got ready to leave, when a plain-looking, chubby woman with no makeup and a bad case of acne answered the door. Her medium-brown hair was short, straight and greasy, her eyes dull and blue.

With an apathetic tone to her voice, the woman said, "Yes?"

"I'm sorry," Arianna stammered, "we must have the wrong house, we're looking for Paula La Paglia."

She looked at them and frowned, "That's me, what do you want?"

Startled, she blurted out, "Oh, okay. Well, I'm Arianna Archer and this is Mike Stevenson from the Meadowville Police Department, can we please come in? We have a few questions for you about your father."

"Sure," she replied listlessly, giving off the impression that she didn't give a crap. She let go of the door, walked into the living room, and sat down on a recliner covered with wrinkled clothes. Paula's house was the mirror opposite of her mother's. It was dirty, messy, and had half-eaten bags of Fritos and Doritos everywhere. The curtains were drawn and all of the lights were off, except one small one, which sat on a little table by the couch. They both sat down gingerly. Arianna, her bug radar on high alert, was manically looking all around her. She HATED bugs, and if she should spot one crawling on her, that would definitively end the questioning for today. She also didn't want to risk contracting something disgusting, like bacterial vaginosis, which is something her annoying neighbor/ex-coworker contracted last year. Arianna didn't actually know how women got that, but she wasn't going to take any chances. She maneuvered her body around precariously, until she was half off the couch and almost falling off. Paula was wearing a ratty yellow robe and slippers, and the house carried an odor of cat urine. That's why I keep Tony and Carmela's litter box in the basement, where it belongs, she thought.

"First off, I am very sorry for the loss of your father."

Paula reacted by mumbling something which sounded like "umm", but could have been, "thanks" out of the corner of her mouth.

"Were you and your father close?" Arianna continued, while pulling her notebook and pen out of her purse. She zipped it up tightly afterwards, not willing to take the chance that something might fly or crawl in there.

"No," she replied sullenly.

"Oh, why not?" Arianna asked, frowning.

"I don't know why it's any of your business, but I'm not close to either of my parents. Although, I do try and make my mother happy by going to church with her, from time to time."

"Can you explain why you're not close to your mother? Believe me, I can relate," she added, nodding her head.

"We're just nothing alike. There was no big feud or anything. I'm sure I was a major disappointment to them. Two beautiful parents and this is what they created," Paula answered, looking down at the floor.

"Oh, you're not that bad, a little cover-up, blush, and mascara would work wonders, I...," her voice trailed off, as Mike had developed a sudden coughing fit. "Anyway, I'm sorry, please continue," Arianna said.

"Both my parents were always smart with money, and made some great investments, but that was one trait I didn't inherit. I don't work, so my parents provide me with a monthly allowance that gives me enough to live on. I'm not good at anything. I'm too stupid to go to college and too ugly to get a husband. My dad tried to get me a job at the design place he worked for, but they said I was too slow and so I was let go."

Wow, what a Debbie Downer, I'm getting depressed just listening to her. "I'm sorry to hear that, it's rough I know, I just recently lost a job myself. However, the reason we're here is, it turns out that your father most likely, did not die of natural causes. We're just trying to figure out exactly what happened," she explained.

"Well, I didn't kill him or anything, if that's why you both are here," Paula replied.

"Nobody's accusing you of anything, but we do need to know where you were that afternoon and evening," Arianna told her.

"I was home of course, where else would I be?" she replied. Arianna sighed and looked over at Mike. Right now, she was second-guessing her request to interview Paula.

Arianna was starting to feel uncomfortable so she shifted, and this time, put all her weight on the back of her right butt cheek, rather than her left. "Paula, did your father ever talk about having any trouble with anyone? Did he have any enemies that you know of?"

"If you're trying to find someone that might have done something like that to my father, you should probably look at Sarah Brewster," she off-handedly suggested.

"Sarah Brewster? Why do you say that?" asked Arianna, a little surprised.

"My dad's supposedly ground-breaking designs and innovative ideas put Sarah's husband's company out of business," Paula replied.

"Oh, her husband's in the interior design business?"

"Was, she's a widow now," Paula explained, "but yes, their two companies were the only ones competing for business around here. This isn't California, you know. It's much harder to make a name for yourself in interior design here in Illinois. From what my father told me, her husband Steve was pretty resentful. Who knows? Maybe Sarah was carrying out some sort of revenge thing on behalf of her husband?"

Arianna closed her notebook and stood up. "Thank you for your time Paula," she said, nodding at Mike. He jumped up, as if he couldn't wait to get the heck out of there. Paula didn't bother walking them out.

The two left her house, and Arianna immediately turned to Mike. "Wow, I bet it's been years since her mother has stepped foot in that house. Paula didn't seem to be too broken up about her father's death, did she?" she remarked.

"I'd have to agree. Hey, not too bad of a job interviewing there, good work," he complimented her. "Especially considering the fact, that you were in," he paused, "a less than ideal environment." She blushed in response to his kind words. "Listen, Riann, I've got some new recruits in and I have to oversee their training. Actually, my plate all around is rather full right now. I think I'd like you to do the legwork and conduct the rest of interviews. In the meantime, I'll do all the research and we'll stay in constant contact with each other, and keep one another in the loop during the course of the investigation. What do you say?"

"That would be fine," she said, trying to affect the world-weary, "I've seen it all" demeanor of a cop and suppressing her elation. She really wanted to prove herself to Mike, so he wouldn't think she was some amateur hack.

He pulled out a short piece of paper out of his left shirt pocket and handed it to her. "Here's a list of the people at the dance who we've determined, had either known Phil and/or had the best opportunity to kill him. Their addresses and phone numbers are also on here."

"Thanks Mike, this will really help," she said, and smiled at him.

"Hey, you want to go somewhere and get some ice cream?" he asked.

"Umm, thanks, but I can't, I'm on a diet," she uncomfortably replied.

"Oh," he said, raising an eyebrow, "does this diet you're on include cookies, and tea with cream and sugar?"

She blushed, but didn't reply. After Mike dropped her off at home, she changed into her "Nurse Jackie" nightgown, which featured the lead character of the hit TV show holding up a hypodermic needle. Arianna made herself comfortable on her pink, floral-patterned couch, that matched two high-backed chairs from the Victorian era which surrounded her cherry wood chess table. The chess table sat in front of a small wood-burning fireplace, which made the whole room come together nicely. She turned on the TV, and as expected, there was absolutely nothing on. Therefore, she turned to her trusty DVR and played an episode of <u>Nurse Jackie</u>.

Arianna loved the show and considered Nurse Jackie someone she'd like to emulate, minus the prescription drug addiction and torrid affair with Eddie her supplier, of course. Whenever she watched the show, it didn't matter whether she was alone or with Mike, Arianna would voice her opinion, that she would have made an excellent nurse, but for the fact that she was grossed out by, in no particular order: urine, feces, blood, old naked people and feet.

However, Arianna did have one beef with the show. She absolutely despised the character of Jackie's oldest daughter, Grace. She believed she was the reason Jackie relapsed all the time. Grace was so incredibly nasty to her mother, that it was very hard for Arianna to watch the show without swearing at the television. Arianna took her TV shows VERY seriously. She'd tell Mike, time and time again, "If I was her mother, I'd be ecstatic if she didn't talk to or live with me! Isn't there some way Jackie could have her relationship with her daughter annulled, on the grounds that Grace is a horrible bitch?" Like he did with most of the ridiculous things that came out of Arianna's mouth, Mike would stifle a laugh and ignore the question. Arianna managed to get through half a <u>Nurse Jackie</u> episode, before she fell asleep with the DVR still playing.

Chapter Five - Stanley

The next morning, Arianna woke up planning to visit the first person on the list that Mike had given her, Stanley Carter, the ancient bartender at the dance. She drove to a small white house with black trim about a mile away from her home. It had a nicely manicured yard that was filled with daffodils and day lilies. Arianna jumped out of her Cavalier, and walked to his front door. She tried both ringing the bell and knocking, but nobody answered. Arianna knew that old people usually have hearing problems, so she rang the bell several more times, knocked even louder, and for good measure, started yelling as well. Unfortunately for Arianna, Stanley Carter's hearing was impeccable, he was just incredibly slow.

He answered the door naked, except for an oversized pair of white boxer shorts. "What?! What the hell do you want?! Stop that infernal racket!"

"Uhh, I am so sorry, I uh, uh." She was having a difficult time speaking because the sight of his pale wrinkly flesh was making her dry heave. Consequently, she was trying to apologize, while at the same time, averting her eyes, which was no easy feat. "Umm, I'm Arianna Archer, a special investigator with the Meadowville Police Department. I was at the St. Francis Singles Dance a couple nights ago and I just wanted to ask you some questions."

"Riann, is that you?" a familiar female voice cried out. Arianna tried to place it, but before her mind could work that fast, Sallie Rigelli, a slender woman of medium height, white porcelain skin, flashing black eyes, and long, shiny, straight black hair stepped out into the hallway behind Stanley, wearing a sheer pink, baby doll nightgown and looking absolutely gorgeous. "I thought that was you!" she squealed, hugging a very startled Arianna.

"Sallie?" she asked, confused.

"Ahh, there's my sweetheart," Stanley said, grabbing and French kissing Sallie.

"My hours got cut at the store, so I have a lot more free time now," Sallie informed her, as if that explained why this old coot's tongue had just been down her throat.

Arianna, hoping she was just having a horrible nightmare, began pinching herself very hard, subsequently yelling, "Ow!" after each pinch.

"Riann, what's wrong? You look like you're going to pass out."

She still couldn't speak, so Sallie led her by the hand to a rocking chair in a small living room, which was exactly what you'd expect an old man's living room to look like. Newspapers spread out all over the coffee table, half a cigar in an ashtray on an end table, a hot water bottle on an old olive-green sofa, and enough pill bottles to fill a pharmacy. Not to mention the fact, that it also reeked of Ben Gay. "Uh you two, you two, are...?"

"Yes, Stanley and I are together. We met each other three weeks ago on LustMatch, and we hit it off immediately," said Sallie.

"Would you like some tea?" Stanley offered, now hovering over Arianna.

"No thanks, do you have something stronger?" she asked.

"Coffee?"

"Stronger," she replied.

"Bourbon?" he asked.

"That'll do the trick," she answered wearily, evidently forgetting that she was there on official business.

"Of course." Stanley left the room, moving at a snail's pace. Arianna watched him closely, feeling as if there was something familiar about him. She knew she had seen him at the dance, but this feeling was different, like he reminded her of someone else. *Oh well, it'll probably come to me later.*

"Sallie, you should really think about putting an age limit on your profile, like under a hundred." Arianna told her, as soon as Stanley was out of earshot.

"Riann, he is the sweetest, funniest guy…," she replied.

Arianna interrupted, "But he's old enough to be your great-great-great-grandfather."

"Riann, he's actually fantastic in bed, you would not believe it…"

"Ugh, please stop!" she cried, putting her hand on her stomach.

Sallie said, "Riann, you don't look too good, are you going to throw up? Can I do anything to help?"

"Yes, actually when Stanley comes back, can you please ask him to put on a shirt, pants, and shoes?"

Sallie gave her a questioning look.

"I'm allergic to the sight of old people's bodies, especially their feet," Arianna explained.

"I didn't know you could be allergic to people," Sallie replied, looking surprised.

"People are allergic to cats and dogs, aren't they? So why not people?"

"Good point," Sallie answered.

"Can you also see where my whiskey is at please?" Arianna requested.

"Sure, I'll be right back," she promised. A minute later, she returned with a shot glass of bourbon. "Sorry, it takes Stanley awhile to get from room to room. I grabbed the drink for you and told him to get dressed. He'll be out in a minute." Arianna gratefully grabbed the drink, downed the bourbon in one shot, and set the glass down on the coffee table. Twenty minutes later, after Sallie had completely nauseated Arianna by giving her a blow-by-blow description, so to speak, of their sex life, Stanley finally returned. Taking two minutes just to cross the room, he sat down on a straight narrow-backed chair in the adjoining dining room.

"There's my little studmuffin!" Sallie cooed. Stanley winked at her in response.

Arianna sighed deeply, fighting back a tidal wave of nausea, and pulled out her pen and notebook. "Stanley, the reason I'm here is because I'm working as a consultant for the Meadowville Police Department on an investigation into Phil La Paglia's death."

Sallie whispered loudly to Stanley, "Arianna is dating the Chief of Police."

"No, I am NOT," she said, sounding exasperated. "Anyway," she continued, "we have reason to believe Phil La Paglia might have been drugged on Friday night."

"Drugged?" he rasped, "and you think I did it?"

"No, not necessarily, we just want to cover all of our bases by getting as much information as possible about what people saw or heard that night," she replied.

"Well, the Chief of Police, oh I'm sorry, your boyfriend," Arianna shot Sallie an annoyed look, "already questioned me last night and I told him I knew nothing. I served Phil a JB and water and that was it," Stanley answered.

"I just knew something bad was going to happen that night," Sallie interrupted. "I told Stanley he should stay home with me and not go, but my Stanley has such a strong work ethic," she said, smiling proudly at him.

Arianna ignored her and asked him, "Who had access to the alcohol besides you?"

"It was all kept in a locked cabinet underneath the bar and I had the key. We only opened it for the Singles Dances," he explained. "If I were you, I'd talk to Sarah. She's the one in charge of all of the Singles Dances and she's the only one who has an extra key to everything."

Arianna was jotting all of this down. "Did you notice anything out of order when you opened the bar that night?"

"Nope, everything looked the same as usual," he told her, scratching his chin thoughtfully.

"Did you leave the bar at any time?"

"Yes, I had to visit the restroom a few times. My prostate…"

Arianna, not wanting to hear about any of his body parts, especially his prostate, raised her hand, swiftly cutting him off. "Did anyone cover for you while you were gone?"

"Yes, actually a few people, Camille, Esther, and Rachel," he said.

"Riann, Stanley is not a murderer!" Sallie cried.

"Sallie please, don't you think you're a little biased? I'm just doing my job, we have to question everyone," she pointed out.

"Riann, remember I have "The Gift," she replied, pointing to her head, referring to the psychic intuition she had inherited from her Italian grandmother on her father's side. Arianna took her gift pretty seriously, for Sallie had predicted last year that something horrific was going to befall Arianna, and soon after, she discovered her extremely annoying, ex-coworker Susie had moved into Arianna's neighborhood. Therefore, respecting "The Gift", she dropped the subject.

"Are you done now Riann?" Sallie asked. "Stanley and I have some unfinished business to attend to," she said, winking at Stanley. Stanley, with a resigned look on his face, appeared exhausted. "Don't worry honey, you can nap afterwards," she assured him.

Arianna started to gag, but recovered quickly. "One last question, how well did you know Phil La Paglia?" Stanley didn't answer. Arianna started to repeat herself, thinking he didn't hear her. "I said, how well did you know…"

He interrupted her, "I heard you. Not hardly at all. I served him drinks at the dances, exchanged pleasantries, that's about it," he answered grumpily.

Standing up, she said, "Well, thank you for your help Stanley. Nice to see you again Sallie, bye!" She ran down the steps and out onto the sidewalk that led to her car. She got in and gagged one more time. *This case is a lot harder, and much more nauseating than I anticipated. I should ask Mike for some more money.* She checked her voice mail and learned she had one message from Mike. She quickly called him back.

"What's up?" she asked, when he picked up on the second ring.

"Riann, we found out a few things you need to know in regards to Phil's finances. Phil died without leaving a will or life insurance policy. It also appears that for the past couple of years, he was making regular monthly payments of a few hundred dollars to Rachel Gordon. Can you ask around about this and see what you can find out?"

"Yeah, no problem. I'll call Arlene, she might know something," she replied. "Oh, and guess what?!"

"What?" he answered.

"Guess who Stanley Carter, the old geezer bartender is dating?"

"Dating?" repeated Mike, sounding surprised. "He could barely move, as I recall."

"SALLIE RIGELLI!" Arianna shouted into her phone.

After Mike's ear stopped ringing, he replied, "You've got to be kidding me!"

"No, I am not, and if that isn't bad enough, when he answered the door today, all he had on was a pair of boxer shorts!"

"Oh no," he said, "did he at least have his feet covered?"

"No!" she wailed.

"Oh man, you must have been going nuts," he replied sympathetically. Mike was very much aware of Arianna's old feet aversion and sincerely felt sorry for her.

"Yep! I had no idea this investigation was going to be so physically and emotionally traumatizing," she told him quite dramatically.

"Oh," Mike said, "by the way, Arlene's story checks out. She was home all afternoon and evening the night of Phil's death."

"Well, that's good," she replied.

"I also delved into the details of their divorce. Arlene initiated it and cited irreconcilable differences. By all accounts, their divorce was an unusually civil one."

"I figured she was telling the truth, but thanks for making sure, Mike."

"No problem. Uh Riann, I gotta go, something just came up here, a domestic disturbance. Some woman had too much to drink and hit her husband over the head with a frying pan."

"Alright, I'll talk to you later." Arianna ended the call and drove home. After she found Arlene's contact information on the list Mike had given her, she gave her a call.

"Hello?" a female voice answered the phone.

"Hi, is this Arlene?" asked Arianna.

"Yes," she replied, "who is this?"

"This is Arianna Archer. I came over the other day with Mike Stevenson to talk to you about Phil."

"Oh yes, of course. Are you calling to schedule the tour I offered you?" she asked cheerfully.

"No, unfortunately, I don't have time for that today. I just have a couple of follow-up questions I was hoping to ask you."

"Certainly, ask away," Arlene replied.

"The police discovered Phil had been making regular monthly payments to Rachel Gordon. Do you know what that was about?"

"Yes, I do. Phil had accidentally rear-ended Rachel a couple of years ago. He hadn't been drinking or anything. He was just driving a little too fast and didn't have enough time to slow down. By the time he did, he hit her and she ended up with a mild case of whiplash and, from what Phil told me, moderate pain in various parts of her body. Phil felt so guilty that he promised Rachel that he would give her money every month. It was my understanding that she refused at first, but he basically forced her to take it. That's the kind of man he was."

Again, Arianna mourned the lost opportunity she could have had with Phil. "Thanks, just one more question. Did you know Phil died without a will?"

"No, I guess we never really discussed it. He would have probably ended up leaving everything to Paula anyway. As it stands now, she will get everything, right?" Arlene asked her.

"That's my understanding," replied Arianna. "Thank you Arlene, I appreciate you clarifying these things for me."

"Not a problem," she replied, "have a good day."

Chapter Six - Sarah

The next day, Arianna called Mike and repeated her conversation with Arlene verbatim.

"Thanks Riann, I'll let you know if we turn up anything else on our end," he replied.

As soon as they hung up, Arianna's sister called her. "Riann, we've found someone perfect for you."

"Oh?" she replied dubiously.

"Yes, Josh is sweet and intelligent and has a good job," Emily told her in a self-satisfied tone.

"Is he tall?" she asked.

"Yes, he's tall. He's heard all about you and I even showed him some pictures."

She winced. "Oh God, I hope you haven't shown him any recent pictures."

"Don't worry, these were from a few years ago, and I think he's already smitten," Emily said, in a high, excited voice.

"Well of course, who wouldn't be?" she replied. Humility was never Arianna's strong suit.

Her sister ignored the arrogant comment. "Well, he wants to take you out tonight," she told her.

"Tonight? Isn't that a little soon?" asked Arianna.

"No, the sooner the better Riann. You're not getting any younger, you know," she said, stating the obvious. Arianna believed that Emily and Sandra probably spent most of their free time counting how many eggs she has left. "Be ready at five," Emily ordered.

"Five? That's really early to go to dinner," she said.

"No, your date is for seven, but mom and I are coming over at five to get you ready."

Get me ready? Oh Lord, this is clearly a fate worse than death. Her mother and sister were bad enough on their own, but together they could really, and they often did, make her life miserable. "Fine," she reluctantly agreed.

"Great, see you later!" Emily signed off enthusiastically.

Arianna got dressed and decided to visit Sarah Brewster who, surprisingly, lived only two blocks away from her house. She specifically wanted to ask Sarah about the liquor cabinet at St. Francis and her late husband's business connection with Phil La Paglia. She thought she'd walk there, not only because it was a beautiful sunny day, but she was also trying to lose the weight she had gained over the last year and a half. Unfortunately, when she arrived, Arianna was all out of breath and sweaty. *Wonderful, me and my bright ideas.* She slowly climbed up the four steps to Sarah Brewster's brown-brick bungalow, while looking frantically through her purse for some gardenia body spray. She rang her doorbell and managed to both find the spray and use it, seconds before a woman with a blond beehive hairdo and cats-eye glasses stuck her head out the door. "Hello, can I help you?"

"Hi, I'm Arianna Archer. I'm working as a consultant for the Meadowville Police Department, in regards to Phil La Paglia's death," she introduced herself. "Can I come in?"

"Oh yes," she nodded, "you're Sandra Archer's girl, the older single one."

Arianna sighed and rubbed her forehead. "Yes, that's right, I just have a few questions concerning Phil and the St. Francis Singles Dances."

"Yes yes, come in," she said, putting her hand on Arianna's shoulder, and leading her into a moderately-sized living room with a small electric fireplace, solid blue loveseat, couch and chair. Sarah was wearing a sleeveless beige blouse and matching Bermuda shorts with white tennis shoes. "Sit down, make yourself comfortable," she gestured towards the loveseat. "Oh God, I still can't believe it, the ladies and I are in shock," Sarah told her.

"The ladies?"

"Yes, Esther, Rachel and Camille. We attend St. Francis Church and we go to all of the Singles Dances. Actually, I'm in charge of the dances," she explained.

"So you knew Phil well?" asked Arianna, while scribbling away in her notebook.

"Yes, Phil, Arlene, and Paula used to attend St. Francis regularly until the divorce. Paula was a teenager, I believe, at the time. Phil joined us a few times a year, while Arlene and Paula go a little more often. To be honest with you, it's pretty clear Arlene is basically forcing Paula to go to church. I'm sure she believes it will help lift herself out of the ten year funk she's been in." Sarah rolled her eyes. "However, Phil has attended many of our Singles Dances since the split-up with Arlene."

While Arianna was writing all of that down as quickly as possible, Sarah said, "You know dear, Phil seemed quite smitten with you. I haven't seen him that attentive to anyone in a long time."

"Really?" she stopped writing and blushed. "Has he had any girlfriends over the years that you recall, since his divorce?"

"Maybe two or three in all these years," Sarah replied.

"That's it? That's not many," Arianna said, sounding surprised.

"To tell you the truth, I don't think he really ever got over Arlene leaving him. She was truly the love of his life."

"By the way," Arianna asked, "what was the name of that awful woman who accused me of being a floozy Friday night?"

"Oh, that's just Esther, Esther Sullivan. She hasn't been at St. Francis that long, maybe six years or so. Don't let her upset you. Last year, her husband left her for a much younger woman and she's still extremely bitter. She dislikes anyone involved in May/December romances," Sarah informed her.

"Well, that certainly explains it," she replied. "Do you know of anyone that might have wished to do Phil harm?" she asked.

"Why would you ask that? Did you find out for certain that Phil didn't die of natural causes?" Sarah asked her, sounding alarmed. "We've all been wondering what exactly happened to him. Phil was relatively young, you know."

"We really don't know anything for sure at this point," Arianna replied. "The tox screen came back inconclusive, and we don't want to jump to any conclusions. We just want to cover all our bases," she added.

"Oh I see, but no, I don't know of anyone who'd want to harm him." She stroked her chin thoughtfully. "Although," she said, after thinking about it a minute, "Paula is very troubled, I wouldn't put anything past her."

"What exactly do you mean by troubled?" Arianna asked, pretending to be ignorant.

"That girl has been a problem for both Phil and Arlene for years. She won't get a job, won't make any friends, doesn't take care of herself or her home. It's ridiculous! She has, well had, two wonderful parents, who would do anything for her, and look at what's she made of her life!" She shook her head. "It's utterly disgraceful; a lot of people would kill to have parents like that." Arianna nodded her head vigorously in agreement.

"Thank you Sarah. Now I'd like to just ask you a couple of questions concerning the liquor cabinet at the dance."

"What would you like to know?" Sarah replied. "Oh God," she said, looking upset, "I hope he wasn't poisoned or anything."

"Stanley Carter told me that only you and he had keys to the cabinet, is that true?" Arianna asked.

"Yes, that's right. Since I'm the one who gets everything prepared for the dances, I unlock the cabinet and serve as bartender on the evenings Stanley can't make it. I'm always the one who locks it back up at night though, since he doesn't like to stay up too late on Friday nights."

"Is there any way somebody could have copied your key?" she asked.

"I don't know. I suppose so, I guess, if they were brash enough to steal my key ring, take the key, make a copy of it, and then put it back," Sarah admitted.

"Hmmm, interesting. Well, I'd better leave soon, I'd like to go visit Rachel Gordon next," said Arianna, standing up.

"I doubt she'll be of any help. Rachel's not much for talking."

"OK, well, thanks for the warning. Are you all looking for men?" she asked, noticing the rows of Harlequin romances in the small oak bookcase in Sarah's living room.

"Heavens no," she said laughing. "I'm widowed, but I'm not in the market. I really don't have the time, nor the inclination. I am quite busy with my two daughters and four grandchildren." She walked over into what appeared to be her bedroom, and quickly returned with a large color photo in a brass frame, featuring Sarah, her two daughters, and four boys, ranging, Arianna guessed, from four to ten years of age.

"What a beautiful family you have," she complimented her.

"Thank you," she replied with a smile. "Esther, as I mentioned before, is divorced and hates men right now. Rachel and Camille are both single, but I don't think I've ever seen either one with a man."

"Did I hear correctly that your husband was in the same line of business as Phil, interior design?" asked Arianna.

"Yes, yes he was. Steve died a few years ago from lung cancer. Was a smoker all his life, and just couldn't kick the habit."

"I had heard there might have been some feud between him and Phil," Arianna said casually.

Sarah's mood immediately darkened, and crossing her arms over her chest, she barked, "Where did you hear that? Oh never mind, the gossip mill always runs rampant in small churches. There really wasn't any feud at all. For the last couple of years that Steve worked, month by month, Phil's business was doing a lot better than his, and so my husband decided to retire early. Good thing he did, because it enabled us to get a couple of good years in together before he died," said Sarah.

"I see. Thanks so much Sarah, I appreciate you talking to me," Arianna said sincerely. *Boy, did she get testy when I brought up her husband; I wonder what that's about.*

"Anytime dear, take care," Sarah replied, as she walked her to the door.

Chapter Seven - Blind Date

Arianna's sister came over at 5 pm on the dot, thankfully without Maxwell. She loved her nephew, but almost every time he visited her, he either vomited or broke something, sometimes even both. Emily, just a shorter, thinner version of Arianna, was carrying a big knapsack with her. Arianna welcomed her inside, then asked what was in her bag.

"Oh, makeup, hair products, that kind of thing," she replied.

"I do have makeup and hair products here you know," Arianna informed her.

Emily just ignored her and emptied out her knapsack onto Arianna's dresser. "OK, we have mascara, eye shadow, blush, concealer, nail polish, curling iron, etc. I also brought this," she said, while holding up what looked to be a big beige unitard.

"What the heck is that?"

"It's a tummy tamer and hips concealer," explained Emily.

"Are you implying that I have something that needs taming or concealing?" Arianna asked, clearly affronted.

"Oh no, no," her sister quickly answered, "I just wanted to provide some options for you on your big date." Arianna glared at her in response.

A few minutes later, the doorbell rang. Arianna sighed deeply and remarked, "Oh lovely, the other half of the <u>What Not to Wear</u> team has arrived. After spending what seemed like an eternity, commenting on how horrible Arianna's wardrobe was, (Arianna still didn't see what was so wrong about leopard prints) her mother and sister settled on a thin, navy blue blouse, matching skirt, and white heels, which did look great against Arianna's tan legs, she had to admit. Being able to lounge around and suntan outside all day long was one of the few benefits being unemployed provided her. Arianna never listened to the naysayers who cautioned everyone about too much sun. She believed any damage it would do in the future was a small price to pay for the attractiveness she believed it brought her now. The only problem with her outfit was that the skirt was too tight, so she was forced to wear the tummy concealing unitard or "Iron Maiden", as Arianna referred to it. She had to admit though, it did allow her to be able to zip her skirt all the way up and breathe at the same time. Two big pluses in Arianna's book. However, the first time she let them do her hair and makeup, she almost burst out crying, because she ended up looking just like "Honey Boo Boo", from The Learning Channel. She ended up shooing them both out of the bathroom, washing all her makeup off, and starting from scratch. As a final touch, she sprayed on Estee Lauder's "Beautiful".

"Oh, you look awesome Riann!" her sister gushed, grabbing her by the upper arms.

Her mother, a little more subdued, said, "You look very nice Arianna." Which, in Sandra Archer speak, was a major compliment.

All of a sudden, they heard a gigantic clap of thunder. Arianna peered out her bedroom window and beheld a dark grey sky accented by several flashes of lightening. Well, this is an ominous sign, she thought.

"OK, thank you for your help, you can go now," she, matter-of-factly, told the both of them. "It looks like there's a bad storm coming, so you better get out while you can," she said, while practically shoving the two women out the door.

"Don't be rude Arianna," her mother admonished.

"Riann, we want to see him pick you up," Emily whined.

"But why?" she asked.

"Because it's so exciting!" her sister gushed.

"Oh boy." Arianna shook her head. "You are way too easily excited, Emily. This isn't a high school prom date. Listen, I would really prefer you both leave now. I'm nervous enough as it is, and I'd like some time alone."

Despite her protests, Arianna managed to shoo her sister out the door within a few minutes. Her mother, unfortunately, was dilly-dallying. By now, it was evident the wind and the rain were coming in full-force that evening. *Oh great, I hope my basement doesn't flood,* she thought. Meadowville, like many other southwest Chicago suburbs, was well-known for its tendency to flood, since it was located precariously close to the Des Plaines River. To her consternation, she heard the sound of the doorbell. "Dammit Mom, he's already here!"

"Don't worry, I'm just leaving," she reassured her, as she picked up her purse. Arianna took a deep breath. *OK, this may be it, the day I meet the man of my dreams. I need to remember this day and write it down so I'll recall it later when we celebrate our future anniversaries.* She opened the door to see a tall man dripping wet, with light brown hair and blue eyes. He had a short beard, an athletic build and a wilted pink rose in his hand.

"Hi," Arianna said, "you must be Josh, come in. This is my mother Sandra, she's just leaving." She looked pointedly at her mother.

"Hello Arianna," he said.

"Oh, call me Riann," she replied.

He looked over at her mother. "Hello Sandra," he said politely.

"It's a pleasure to meet you Josh, but if you want some advice, don't go dancing with her. The last guy who did ended up in a body bag," Sandra Archer said, opening up her umbrella as she flounced out the door. Josh stood there with a stricken look on his face.

"Just ignore her," Arianna told him, "I'll get my purse and we can go."

"OK. Oh, this is for you," he said, handing her the rose, "it looked much better before the wind and the rain got a hold of it," he told her ruefully.

"Oh, that's all right. Thank you, I'll go put this in a glass of water as well, I'll be right back." She returned within a minute and walked out with him, pulling and locking the front door behind her.

"You look nice Riann," he yelled over the rain, as she quickly followed him over to his car.

"Thank you Josh, so do you," she yelled back.

"Well, this is our ride," he pointed to a nice black, safe-looking automobile, which was NOT a sports car, Arianna was delighted to see. He ran around and opened her door for her and then swiftly ran back and ducked into the driver's seat, slamming the car door. "I thought we'd go to Sam's Steakhouse, would that be all right with you?"

She perked up. "Of course," she replied. Visions of large, juicy, well-aged steaks filled her head, as well as the humongous chocolate lava cake they offered for dessert. Needless to say, all concern about her diet had disappeared. For the rest of the ride, an awkward silence ensued. Arianna was waiting for Josh to start the conversation, for she had been told in the past that she tended to overly dominate conversations. Actually, she was told she talked too much, but Josh was either too shy or had nothing to say. Luckily, Sam's Steakhouse was only fifteen minutes away. There was now quite a torrential downpour outside, and after making a mad dash across the parking lot, by the time they arrived at the restaurant, they were pretty much soaked. Surprisingly, for a fine dining establishment, Sam's had no valet parking unfortunately, and Arianna rarely used or carried umbrellas. Mainly because, by the time she was actually able to get an umbrella open, quite often she was already at her destination and it always took her twice as long to close it up.

After the couple dashed into the restaurant, they were quickly seated at their table by a young, pretty blond hostess, dressed in a crimson red silk dress. Arianna asked Josh, "Have you ever been here before?"

"No, but Bill recommended it," he replied. Good, she thought, Emily must have told him how much I love this restaurant. "What do you do for a living Arianna?" he asked.

"Well, currently I'm helping the Meadowville Police Department with a case," she replied. "They hired me as a consultant."

"Oh," he asked, raising an eyebrow, "how did that happen?"

At that moment, a beautiful red-headed waitress, wearing an expensive-looking black suit, approached their table interrupting them, "Good evening, welcome to Sam's Steakhouse. My name is Karen. Would you like a drink to start off with?"

Josh looked at Arianna, and she shook her head. "No, thank you," he told her. The waitress looked over at Arianna and gave her a funny look. Arianna noticed this, but then just chalked it up to her overactive imagination.

"Alright, well I will be back then in a few minutes to take your order. Take as much time as you need." She smiled and walked away.

Arianna picked up the conversation where they had left off, "You heard about the death at St. Francis a few nights ago, right?"

"No, I don't think I have," he answered.

"Oh? It was in all the local papers."

"I don't read much," he responded.

"Oh." Arianna's mood darkened. "Anyway, last year I had solved two murders at St. James Christian Church that were thought to be deaths due to natural causes."

"Oh, good job then," he said. Another awkward silence followed.

Their waitress Karen came back to the table. "Hello folks, are you ready to order now?" They both ordered filet mignons with baked potatoes and sour cream and Caesar salads. When Arianna handed her menu back to the waitress, again, she could have sworn the waitress was staring at her funny.

"So, you work with Bill?" Arianna asked, now trying desperately to make conversation.

He explained, "Yes, we've worked together for the last five years. We're in the blah blah blah department at blah blah," which is exactly how Arianna heard it, for it was all so boring to her. She hadn't even realized he had stopped talking. Luckily, just then they received their salads, so the both of them were able to solely focus on eating for the next several minutes.

Arianna's right eye started to blink rapidly. She figured she might have a lash in there, so she dug around in her purse for her compact. She opened up the compact and yelped loudly. "Oh my God, I look like a fricken raccoon!" she cried out, mortified. Mascara had run down her face and there were deep black circles under her eyes, not to mention black streaks on her cheeks. She glanced over at Josh, and noticed he was behaving rather awkwardly. "Why didn't you tell me that I look like this?!" she asked him, obviously irked.

"Well, I didn't want to make you feel uncomfortable," he mumbled, nervously shifting in his seat.

"So you don't think I feel uncomfortable now, looking ridiculous in front of you, the hostess, the customers? Oh my gosh, no wonder that waitress kept looking at me funny!" She gave a long sigh. *Mike would have told me immediately, that's for damn sure.* She took the white cloth napkin off her lap and dipped it into her water glass, attempting to wash as much mascara off her face as possible.

After Arianna had calmed down, she suddenly had a thought. "So Josh, what kind of music do you like?" she asked, leaning in closer.

"Oh, anything really," he replied.

"Anything?" she answered, mildly irked.

"Yes," he said.

"OK, how about gangsta rap, do you like that?"

"Gangsta what?" He seemed confused.

"Gangsta rap," she repeated, louder and clearer.

"Uh, no," Josh replied.

"Then I guess you don't like ALL music, do you?" Again, there was uncomfortable silence, which was thankfully broken by the waitress, Karen arriving with their steaks. Arianna was pleased; her steak was absolutely, mouthwateringly delicious. After she finished most of her dinner, Arianna took a deep breath, OK, last chance buddy, she thought. "What are your favorite TV shows?'

"TV? Oh, I don't watch TV," he told her.

"Whaaat?!" Arianna almost fell off her chair.

"I actually don't own a television; I feel it's just a major time waster."

Arianna frantically flagged their waitress down, "Check please!"

"Won't you be ordering any dessert?' he asked, a little startled.

"No, that won't be necessary," she answered. Even thoughts of chocolate lava cakes dancing in her head weren't enough for her to move forward with this debacle. She got the rest of her food wrapped to go, and they left soon after Josh paid the check. When they had first entered the restaurant, a very peppy teenage girl working the coat room, had offered to take Arianna's jacket, but she refused. Arianna didn't believe in willingly giving strangers her coat, or luggage, or anything else, for that matter. She let anyone who asked know, that she didn't trust people not to lose or give away her things to the wrong person. However, the real reason she was averse to handing over her stuff, was that Arianna completely lacked patience. She hated having to wait for someone to fetch her bags or jacket, before she could unpack or leave. This quirk of hers came in handy that night, since she had persuaded Josh not to check his jacket either, and; therefore, they were both able to leave immediately after paying the bill.

The rain still hadn't let up at all, and so they were forced to, once again, run to his car, trying as much as possible to avoid getting wet. To Arianna's dismay, it took Josh forever to get her home, because he kept taking longer side routes to avoid huge standing puddles of water in the road. She was rapidly losing her patience. Arianna yelled, "You could have made that one!" when he refused to drive down a semi-flooded street that would have got her home in a couple of minutes. Instead, he put his car into reverse and took another route, completely out of the way. Josh didn't bother defending himself, for like Arianna, he was quite tired, wet, and cranky.

When they finally reached her house, he walked, or actually, ran Arianna to her front door. She thanked him, and before he could even try and kiss her goodnight, she had swiftly opened the door, walked into the house, and slammed it in his face. Afterwards, she quickly undressed and threw her clinging wet clothes down the stairs into the basement. She took a long hot shower, got into her PJs, and had somewhat calmed down, before she called her sister.

As soon as Emily picked up the phone, Arianna let her have it. "Are you high? What the hell would ever possess you to think I would actually be a match with Josh?"

"Why? What happened? What's wrong?" she answered, alarmed.

"What's wrong? What's NOT wrong? He has no personality to speak of, nil, zip, nada, and is possibly the worst conversationalist of all time, and worst of all, he doesn't even own a television set!" Arianna was using exaggerated hand gestures to accentuate her speech, something she did automatically whenever she was angry.

"You are just too picky Riann," Emily calmly replied.

"Too picky?" she repeated incredulously. "Yeah, too picky to actually think I might want to occasionally be able to talk to the man of my dreams." Emily looked up at her kitchen ceiling and sighed deeply in response. "Do me a favor Emily, don't try and set me up anymore, it's not even worth the free dinner!" Before her sister could even reply, she ended the call and snuggled into bed with Tony and Carmela. "We don't need a man anyway, do we?" The two cats purred in response. She turned on the TV and began switching channels rapidly, trying to find something worth watching. Arianna became gleeful when she found an episode of <u>Wonder Woman</u> on MeTV.

Arianna always experienced a wave of nostalgia while watching the show. As a child, she loved <u>Wonder Woman</u>. She was only one year-old or so, when the original series was on the air, but she'd been introduced to the show during its years in syndication. She loved the character of Wonder Woman so much, that she begged her mom for a pair of Wonder Woman Underoos as a kid. After her mother relented and bought her the Underoos, she'd wear them constantly and refuse to take them off. In fact, she'd throw a tantrum if her parents tried to make her change her clothes. They finally gave up and let her have her way one summer, until they noticed an unpleasant odor wafting through their house. Under protest, (she tried to blame the smell on the dog) Arianna was unceremoniously plopped inside the bathtub, and her Underoos swiftly thrown into the washing machine.

One of the gifts Wonder Woman had was a magic "golden lasso" which, when thrown over someone, would give her the power to force them to tell the truth. Arianna would take her own "golden lasso" (crappy old jump rope) and throw it around her sister Emily. She'd then command Emily to tell her the truth when she asked a specific question, which, for example, could be, "did she or did she not steal Arianna's favorite Barbie doll?" Her mother had quickly become tired of constantly yelling at Arianna to untie her little sister. She would also be annoyed, because Arianna would waste all of her aluminum foil. Her eldest daughter would take the foil and wrap it around her wrists, in order to replicate Wonder Woman's silver bracelets which enabled her to deflect bullets. Her mother found this extremely embarrassing, especially when she'd be in the middle of hosting a Tupperware party and Arianna would walk through in her Underoos, thrusting her crossed wrists outwards, deflecting imaginary bullets. Her mother would react by pretending that she wasn't actually there, hoping that the ladies would think she was just some odd neighbor girl who made herself at home in their house from time to time.

If that weren't bad enough, Arianna would often spin around and around extremely fast, just like Diana Prince did in order to change into Wonder Woman. Arianna would whip off her glasses, which would literally rend her as blind as a bat, and start spinning like a top all over the living room. Unfortunately, she'd spin herself around so much that she'd get quite dizzy and fall down on the floor with a loud thud. Once, she even knocked over an expensive lamp in the living room. Another time, she broke her mother's favorite vase. Probably the worst thing she ever did; however, was when she spun around and fell on top of her little white poodle, Keith Partridge. Arianna was a pretty chubby kid, so she almost crushed the poor dog to death. That was the last straw for her mother, and shortly afterwards Sandra Archer forbade any simulation of super heroes in the house. *Ahh, memories…*

Chapter Eight - Rachel

The next morning, Arianna was at home and looking through her notes, when her cell phone buzzed in the pocket of her skin-tight blue jeans. Of course, all of her jeans were tight these days. She had been contemplating just telling people she was pregnant, but wasn't sure if she wanted to deal with all the repercussions, namely all the questions people would have when she failed to produce a baby in nine months. She squeezed the phone out and saw that it was Mike. "Yes?"

"Hi Riann, just checking in to see how the investigation is going."

"It's going pretty well. I was able to question Sarah Brewster and I plan on visiting Rachel Gordon next."

"Learn anything useful?" he asked.

"Well, Sarah played down the feud angle in regards to her husband and Phil. She actually got a little snippy when I brought it up. However, I did find out that, though improbable, it would be possible for someone to steal her key, or even Stanley's key for that matter to the liquor cabinet, make a copy and then return it. I'm afraid that's all I got so far."

"Well, that's a good start," said Mike. "By the way, how was your date last night?" he said in an overly casual tone.

"Date?" she asked.

"You heard me," he replied, his voice now betraying his anger.

She began to wave her hands about. "How did you know I went on a date last night? Have you been talking to my mother?" She paused, waiting for him to respond. "Wait, are you stalking me?" clearly outraged, she accused him.

"Of course not, I'm a cop, I know these things," Mike replied, offended.

"Uh huh," Arianna said, furious.

"Actually, one of my men saw you at Sam's Steakhouse," he admitted.

"Oh great, and he just had to report to you every detail of my private life? What are you guys, TMZ??" she replied, obviously upset.

"Don't you think you're being a little melodramatic?" he asked.

"No, and I hate when you accuse me of that!"

"Well, when it walks like a duck and quacks like…," he replied.

She cut him off, "I don't have time for this Mike, I'm very busy and on my way to question Rachel Gordon."

"OK, but you never answered my question, how was your date?"

"Why don't you just ask one of your men?" Arianna replied. "Gotta go, bye," she said, quickly ending the call and slipping her phone back into her pocket.

She walked out the door and over to her car. Soon, she pulled up to Rachel Gordon's little white picturesque house on the corner of Manchester and Villa Avenues. There were two black flower boxes under each front window, displaying pretty pink and purple petunias. Arianna spotted Rachel right away in her backyard hanging up clothes on the clothesline. Huh, I didn't think people did that anymore, she said to herself. She had very fond memories of hanging up clothes with her grandmother years ago in the backyard at the house her mother grew up in.

Rachel was short and stocky, with dark blond, graying hair and blue eyes. She was wearing a cute pink apron around her waist with one big pocket in the middle, which contained a bunch of clothespins.

Arianna noticed her wincing as she reached above her head to hang a housedress on the line. "Hello," she called out loudly, startling her.

"Oh my Lord, you scared me," Rachel answered, her hand on her heart. She looked at Arianna closely. "You're the woman from the dance," she said in a soft, pleasant voice.

"Yes, that's right. I'm Arianna Archer," she introduced herself, switching her notebook to her left hand, and extending her right, "nice to meet you." Rachel shook her hand and then looked at her quizzically.

"I was hoping you could tell me a little bit about what went on at the St. Francis Singles Dance on the night Phil La Paglia died."

"Why?" she answered, confused.

"Well, the police have reason to believe that Phil La Paglia may have been drugged, and I'm helping them out as a consultant in the investigation into his death."

"Drugged?" Rachel seemed genuinely upset. She sat down slowly and carefully on one of the two white chairs with green polka-dotted seat cushions, that were set up on her outside patio.

"We have reason to believe he might have been drugged or poisoned at the dance," she revealed.

"How?" Rachel asked.

"We're not sure yet," she answered. "How well did you know Phil?" Arianna asked her.

"Really not much at all, just from the St. Francis Singles Dances and a few times greeting him at church over the years."

"Hmm, interesting," Arianna responded. "Did you notice anyone acting suspicious the night of the dance?" she asked her.

Rachel looked up at the sky and thought for a very long minute. "No, I don't think so, except that Stanley seemed to be spending a lot of time in the bathroom."

"That's right, Stanley mentioned that you, Esther, and Camille subbed as bartender for him while he was in the bathroom. Is that true?"

"Yes," she replied.

"How many times did you cover for him, Rachel?"

"Twice."

Arianna sighed. *I have a feeling this is going to be like pulling teeth.* "Do you remember what time it was when you subbed for him?"

"Once, it was pretty early in the evening, and the other time was a couple of hours later, but I don't remember the exact times."

"And while you were covering for him, were you called away at any time?"

"No, I wasn't."

"Well, I have to run. By the way," Arianna asked, "just curious, what do you do for a living?"

"I was a retired schoolteacher, but now I'm a tutor. I work with children after school lets out at 4 pm, Monday through Thursday," said Rachel.

"Thank you Rachel, you've been very helpful. I'm planning on interviewing Camille...," she rifled through her notes, "Ciccone next. Ciccone, is that Italian?"

"Yes, it's Sicilian," she replied.

"Interesting, Phil had mentioned he was Sicilian. I didn't know there was such a big Italian population here, let alone Sicilian. My friend Sallie Rigelli is Sicilian too."

"Oddly enough, Phil's family and Camille's family both come from the same small town in Sicily. I remember Camille talking about it once. There was some big scandal or something between the two families resulting in a huge feud."

"Wow, that's certainly interesting," Arianna replied. "Oh Rachel, one more thing. I know you said you barely knew Phil, but I thought I heard somewhere that you two were involved in a car accident?"

"True, but that doesn't mean I know him well," she replied.

Arianna asked her, "How badly hurt were you in the accident?"

"Well, I had whiplash, which, thankfully, is gone now. Also, some aches and pains, but nothing major. Because it was his fault, Phil felt guilty every time he saw me, and insisted on writing me checks every month for my pain and suffering. I told him it wasn't necessary, but he begged me to take the money." Rachel looked at Arianna as if she really wanted her to believe what she was saying. Arianna noticed that, although she collaborated nicely what Arlene told her, Rachel seemed to be in more pain than she was letting on.

"Thank you for your time Rachel, I very much appreciate it."

Rachel stood up slowly, wincing a little. "You're welcome," she replied, as she dug into her apron pocket and pulled out another clothespin.

Chapter Nine - Camille

Arianna drove directly from Rachel's house to Camille Ciccone's apartment. She thought she'd save Esther the bitch, for last. Camille lived the farthest of the suspects, about a half hour away in Pinewood Park. She rented an apartment which included a small balcony on the second floor. A tall, thin, morose woman with medium-brown wavy hair and brown eyes, wearing a long-sleeved white blouse and black slacks, answered the door.

"Can I help you?" she asked.

"Yes, I'm Arianna Archer. I'm working with the Meadowville Police Department on an inquiry into the death of Phil La Paglia."

"I don't understand, I thought he had some sort of epileptic fit or something. I was in the bathroom when it happened," she said, sounding a bit aggravated.

"He did have some convulsions, but we're still not sure what caused his death. He may have been drugged or poisoned," she explained.

"Well, I was just about to take a walk," Camille said, slightly annoyed, appearing not to be too upset that Phil might have been murdered.

"Is it okay if we chat for a few minutes?" she asked her.

"I guess I don't have a choice," Camille replied shortly, opening the door a little wider. *Wow, she's a real charmer. This investigation is getting old, really fast.* Arianna unenthusiastically pulled her notebook out and placed it on Camille's small beige kitchen countertop.

"If somebody did drug Phil, who do you think would be the most likely?" Arianna asked.

She wrinkled her brow and thought for a long while. "They always say watch out for the quiet ones, so Rachel, I suppose."

Surprise registered on Arianna's face, but she diligently wrote that down in her notebook. "Stanley tells me you covered for him as bartender during the dance."

"Yes, that's correct," she answered curtly.

"How many times?"

"Twice, I believe." Camille began pacing back and forth, appearing quite jittery.

Arianna jotted that down and asked, "When you tended bar for him, do you recall what time it was?"

She thought a minute, "No, I can't remember."

"Did anyone distract you or take you away from your post at all?" she asked her.

"No," Camille answered, sounding surly.

"How long have you attended St. Francis Church, Camille?"

"About eight years," she answered.

Arianna looked her in the eye. "And you're single?"

"I don't see why that's important, but yes," Camille replied.

"Did you know the La Paglias well?" Arianna questioned her.

"I didn't know Arlene and the daughter well at all. When I came to St. Francis, Phil and his wife were already divorced."

"But Phil?"

"We worked on a project together once," Camille explained.

"What type of project?" asked Arianna, curious.

"I'm a secretary, right now I'm actually on vacation, and Phil needed some typing done for his job. I guess the secretary there went on maternity leave, so he asked if I could help out." While Camille was talking, Arianna looked around and noticed a massive collection of Agatha Christies in her bookcases, as well as, several anthologies of American and British poetry. In her modest living room there was a small desk with a computer on it and a little table with an old typewriter. There was no couch or loveseat, just the two chairs the women were sitting in.

"Did Phil have any enemies that you know of?" she asked.

"I have no idea, we weren't close," she said coldly, pressing her lips together tightly.

"Thank you for your help," Arianna said, closing her notebook.

Camille stared at her. "I'd like to take my walk now, if you don't mind."

"Of course, have a good day," Arianna replied, walking over to the door.

Camille nodded, let Arianna out and then briskly shut the door behind her. As Arianna walked down the steps to leave, Mike called her. "Any progress?" he asked.

"Eh, just finishing up the interviews with Rachel and Camille. I have no real feel yet for who the killer could possibly be, Mike. I just finished talking to Camille and she seems so cold, and it was difficult getting anything useful out of Rachel. Can you please check something out for me though? Rachel did mention that there was an old feud between the La Paglia and the Ciccone families back in Sicily, and I'd just like to see if there's anything to it."

"You think it could be a motive for murder? These Sicilian vendettas can go on for generations, even stretching into other countries."

"I don't know, maybe. It's kind of frustrating, I feel as if we're not progressing too far on this case at all. None of the suspects are saying anything that's really helpful, in my opinion," she said, discouraged.

"Well, it takes time, so try and be patient and don't give up," he said encouragingly.

"Oh, I just remembered, do you know when Phil La Paglia's wake is set for?" she asked.

"No, I do know it's being delayed until the medical examiner is through with the body."

"Oh, OK. Speaking of that, I was thinking maybe we're jumping to the wrong conclusion that Phil was drugged."

"What do you mean?" he asked.

"Well, there are other methods of murder which may not be readily apparent, like a poisoned dart, for example."

"A poisoned dart," he repeated.

"Yeah, a poisoned dart. In the book <u>Death in the Air</u>, the murder weapon was a poisoned dart. You should tell the medical examiner to look for a tiny mark or hole, which could be a point of entry on his body."

"Let me guess, <u>Death in the Air</u> is an Agatha Christie?" Mike was well aware of Arianna's Agatha Christie obsession. He had never read any of her books though, despite Arianna's constant pleading with him to do so. His main defense was that he didn't need to read about crime, he fought against it all day long.

"Of course," she replied.

"Well, I highly doubt he was killed by a poisoned dart, but I promise not to take the possibility off the table, how's that?"

Arianna grumbled. "It doesn't necessarily have to be a poisoned dart, you know. You should ask him to look for any fang marks as well, like from a snake."

He rolled his eyes. "A snake?"

"Hey, haven't you ever read the Sherlock Holmes story, 'The Adventure of the Speckled Band'?"

"Nope."

"You know, Phil was a BIG Sherlock Holmes fan…"

"Well, Phil is dead, look what good that did him," Mike told her.

"Mike, you're so mean!" she replied, aghast, "If it wasn't for the character of Sherlock Holmes, there wouldn't be the forensic science that we have today."

"Riann, don't worry, if Phil was bitten it would have definitely been noticed during the medical examination. Now, not to change the subject or anything, but I'm thinking of watching Season One of Homeland tonight." Mike remarked.

"You are?" she incredulously replied.

"Yeah well, you're always raving about it; I thought I might as well give it a shot."

"Cool," Arianna responded, very pleased. Homeland was one of the TV shows that had previously been on her "banned" list. Arianna couldn't stand one of the characters named Dana, and they kept showing more and more of her each week, until she couldn't take it any longer. She stopped watching it and even wrote the producers of the show, strongly suggesting they kill off her character. Soon after, even though Dana didn't die a gruesome death like Arianna had preferred, her character did move out of the family home and thus, her screen time was cut to almost nothing. Arianna was sure this was due to her brilliantly written letter winning over the writers and producers. The squeaky wheel always gets the grease, she thought triumphantly.

"You're welcome to come watch it with me if you want, you know, to provide any insights or whatever…," Mike offered.

"Well," she paused, "seeing that we're now co-workers and all, sure, why not."

"Great, you want to come over at 8:00?"

"Sounds good, see you then," she replied, ending the call.

At precisely 8 pm, she knocked on the door of Mike Stevenson's small, red, two-bedroom brick ranch house in Meadowville. Arianna still had a key to his house, but she never used it, primarily because she was afraid of what she might walk in on. She and Mike were not exactly a couple at the moment, and it was within his rights to bring a woman home, but even so, she knew she would not handle it well if he did.

"Hey there," he greeted her as she walked in the door. Mike was looking good, wearing tight new blue jeans, a black Dago T-shirt, and black leather shoes, topped off with a hint of "Blue Seduction" cologne. *Damn, I'm in trouble.* Arianna was wearing her blond hair in a long ponytail tied with a white scrunchie and sporting a red t-shirt with white letters that read, "Vote for Pedro", faded blue jeans and gym shoes. He looked her up and down and remarked, "You look nice." For a second, she thought he was being sarcastic, then she realized he was serious.

"Oh, OK thanks," she replied, suddenly feeling unsure of herself.

He said, "I just loaded the DVD, do you want anything to drink?"

"Uh, I'm watching my weight, just water please," she replied, while making herself comfortable on his sofa, looking all around her. Mike, for the most part, tended to be attracted to women who were on the voluptuous side, and Arianna swore that when they were seriously dating, he would sabotage her diet by leaving chocolate turtles and fudge brownies around the house. Therefore, she knew she had to be on high chocolate alert while she was in his house.

"Are you sure?" he asked.

"Umm, well maybe you can put some lemon in it and some sugar?" she said tentatively.

"In other words, you want lemonade?"

"Well, yes I guess so," she replied, slightly embarrassed.

"Sure." He smiled and went and brought her the drink.

She sized up her surroundings and didn't spot anything chocolate around, so she breathed a sigh of relief, although there was a little part of her, she had to admit, that was disappointed. There also seemed to be no evidence of any lady friend hanging around there recently. His house was reasonably clean, but pretty messy. Mike hired a woman to come in once a week and it was evident that she hadn't been there for days. "What day does Natalia come over?" she asked.

"Tomorrow," he replied.

Aha, she thought.

For a moment, Arianna's eyes fell upon a very old picture of Mike and his dad that was displayed in a small silver frame on the coffee table. It was taken in 1985 when Mike was twenty-two years old. You wouldn't know upon looking at it, that it was Mike at first, he was extremely skinny and had layers of dishwater blonde hair. However, if you looked closely enough you would recognize the piercing blue eyes that still managed to captivate Arianna almost thirty years later. The father and son had their arms around each other's shoulders. They were also wearing Chicago Bears "Super Bowl" sweatshirts and grinning from ear to ear. Even though Mike and his father didn't share much in common, the one thing that did always manage to bring them together was the Bears.

His dad, Kenneth Anderson was a huge Bears fan. He took part in tailgating parties and watched every Sunday game at a local neighborhood bar with a rambunctious crowd of Bears fans. He was a big burly guy with the same dishwater blonde hair as his son, and a Mike Ditka style mustache. His father's friends would comment all the time on how much he resembled Ditka. Truth be told, Kenneth Anderson took a lot of pride in looking like the Coach's taller younger brother.

He had been an electrician and had died from a massive heart attack the following year, at the young age of forty-nine while re-wiring a customer's house. Mike always said he was glad his father lived long enough to see the Bears win the Super Bowl. He also lived just long enough to see his oldest son graduate *magna cum laude* from Northern Illinois University with a degree in criminal justice. Mike was grateful for the fact that his dad was right there to watch him join the police force right after college. His family had known Mike had always wanted to be a cop. He had told Arianna that he had been fascinated by police cars since he was four, specifically mesmerized by the flashing red light on top. Truth be told, Mike was a damn good cop. He was smart and tough, but fair, and practically everyone with whom he came into contact, knew he was a straight shooter and soon garnered a deep respect for him.

Mike pressed play on the remote as he sat down next to her on the sofa, which was covered in a light and dark blue checkered pattern. It perfectly matched his blue recliner and the small navy blue rug that covered a tiny portion of his hardwood floor. Arianna was really enjoying herself. She loved explaining to Mike every nuance of Homeland and why, in her opinion, it was so brilliant. After it was over, she turned and expectantly looked at him. "Well?"

Mike nodded and smiled. "It was pretty good, I have to admit," he said.

"Ha!" she exclaimed, "I knew you would love it!" Nothing gave Arianna more pleasure than to turn someone on to a TV show or mystery novel. Mike suddenly reached out and put his hand on her knee. She tried to ignore it, but his Antonio Banderas, "Blue Seduction" was too enticing. When he turned to kiss her, Arianna's brain told her to resist, but her body was advising her to succumb. As usual, Arianna ignored her brain. After a couple of minutes, she pulled away.

"Wait," she said, putting her hand up, "isn't this going to complicate our working relationship?"

"How so?"

"Well, isn't this considered sexual harassment or something?" Arianna said.

"Riann, I'm not your boss. Technically, like me, you also work for Ed, and I would hardly say I'm harassing you, am I?"

"Yeah OK, but won't it complicate things?" She got up and started pacing.

"Tell me how it would complicate things," he said.

"Like for example, what if we're investigating together and some hot guy hits on me and you get all jealous and punch his teeth out?"

Mike rolled his eyes and replied, "I'll take my chances." He stood up and they began kissing again, until Mike stopped and said, "Stay the night?"

"I want to, but I really can't. All I have on my mind right now is this investigation, and I really just want to take some time to be alone to think, OK. Please don't be mad. Besides, the TV show, Sex Brought Me to the ER has pretty much freaked me out about sex, for like, the rest of my life." She closed her eyes, and shuddered just thinking about it.

"What kind of show is that? Boy, the trash they have on TV now is ridiculous," he said with disgust.

"Well, the last thing I need is to find myself in the emergency room with my private parts all hideously swollen, or green, or on fire, or whatever, and having to explain that to my mother and Emily."

Wisely, Mike said nothing. He knew Arianna's tendency to freak out, worry, and become overly dramatic. He decided to just ride it out and kissed her on the forehead before walking her to the front door. "Go home and get some rest, Riann, and maybe try to lay off the TV watching for a while." There was no one more aware of the extent of Arianna's television addiction than Mike.

"Hey, I learn a lot from TV!" she responded, feeling a little bit insulted.

"Yeah, like what?"

"Well, just the other day I learned from, I think ABC News, that when encountering a bear, in order to survive you shouldn't run, but instead, start shouting, clapping your hands, throwing things, and making lots of noise to scare him away. You should also make yourself appear as tall as possible. See, if you act frightened and run away or lie down and get in a fetal position, the bear will treat you like prey and devour you," she explained.

"That's great advice Riann, how many times have you actually encountered a bear in the suburbs of Chicago?" he asked sarcastically.

"That's not the point! You can never be too prepared or too careful."

"I get it, I get it. You're pretty cute, you know that doncha," he told her, while gently moving her hair off her face and stroking her left cheek.

"Good night Mike," she said, smiling bashfully before turning away.

"Good night cutie." He stood outside watching her until she made it safely inside her car.

Arianna was about to put her key in the ignition, when a black Porsche drove up and parked in Mike's driveway. *That's Barbara, what the hell is she doing here?*

Barbara Bingham was Mike's ex-wife. They had divorced twenty years ago, a few years before Arianna met him. Barbara was Arianna's opposite in every way. She was thin and petite, had short dark hair and brown eyes and closely resembled Audrey Hepburn. She was also quiet and subdued, smart and well-educated. She and Mike had met at Northern Illinois University. She was a year younger and pursuing her degree in business administration. Mike and Barbara were married for seven years. While they were married, Barbara snagged a high paying job working for some corporate firm, which required her to do a lot of international traveling. Mike didn't appreciate seeing his wife only once every week and a half or so, and initiated the divorce. She recently remarried some guy named Carlos, who she had met on a trip to South America a few years back.

Arianna had met Barbara several times over the years, as they had occasionally run into each other when Mike and Arianna would visit Mike's brother Matt in Somerset Hills. Barbara lived only a block away from Matt. She was nice enough, but Arianna never failed to feel like a giant klutz in her presence. In addition, Arianna had always assumed that all men badmouthed their ex-wives, but Mike never did. In fact, he rarely ever mentioned her at all, only when they'd run into each other or when Arianna would ask questions about her. This made Arianna wary and a little jealous of her. Barbara was the only long-term serious relationship Mike ever had, except for Arianna. He had one girlfriend in college before Barbara, that only lasted a few months and wasn't serious. After his divorce, he dated a few women, none of which lasted over a month, until he met Arianna.

Mike was still standing outside with a puzzled expression on his face, waiting for Barbara to exit her vehicle. Arianna made a show of digging in her purse for something, in order to delay leaving. Barbara got out of the car wearing a long thin peach dress and white sandals.

She had on a minimal amount of makeup and was sporting a new pixie haircut, which really flattered her face. Arianna watched as Mike smiled, said a few words to her, and then let her inside his house, his right hand on her upper back while walking her inside. *Arrgh, he's touching her. Crap, I should have just stayed the night!*

Arianna decided to go ahead and pretend to leave, but then actually double back and park a half a block down to see what time Barbara left. Unfortunately, an hour later she fell asleep, and woke up startled by a dog howling in the middle of the night. "Dammit!" she cried. She started up the car and headed over to Mike's house. *Please make her car be gone, please make her car be gone. Oh thank God!* To Arianna's immense relief, Barbara Bingham's Porsche was, indeed, gone.

Chapter Ten - Esther

The next morning, Arianna was tired, cranky, and worried. Maybe Barbara came over to Mike's all the time, how would she know? The Columbian dude might have dumped her and Barbara realized what a great catch Mike was, and so was deliberately trying to snatch him away from her. Arianna had, what you'd call, a hyperactive imagination. She was already picturing the both of them in Mike's bed, him force-feeding her Fannie May's, "Mint Meltaways", while they discussed some highbrow subject like international finance or capitalism. Also, today Arianna was going to interview Esther Sullivan, and she was not looking forward to it. She knew that there's nothing worse than dealing with a woman done wrong. Esther, it turned out, lived in a very nice condo in Somerset Hills, not too far from where Arlene La Paglia lived. She was a little worried because something told her that she wouldn't be welcomed with open arms. She decided she'd cross that bridge when she came to it. After consuming a breakfast of Cheerios and Dr. Pepper, Arianna hopped into her car and ten minutes later, arrived at Esther's condo building. She went through the main doors and walked into a spacious entryway that smelled like roses. She saw there was an array of buzzers next to a bunch of last names. She drew a deep breath and pressed the one next to Sullivan.

A minute later, a nasty voice blasted over the intercom. "Yes?"

"Hello Esther, this is Miss Archer, a consultant for the Meadowville PD," she announced, trying to sound as professional as possible. There was no response on the other end. She added, "We're investigating the death of Phil La Paglia and I'd like to talk to you." There was still no response, but the door began buzzing and a few seconds later, Arianna was able to gain entry to the building. Esther's condo was on the first floor, and she only had to walk a short distance before she found her door. She had barely finished knocking once, when Esther yanked open the door, startling her.

"Oh, it's you!" she exclaimed, looking as if she just smelled something bad. Esther was a short redhead with freckles and dark blue eyes. She was a little on the chunky side and was wearing a billowy emerald green blouse and blue jeans. Arianna noticed she was barefoot and that her fire engine red toenails matched her fingernails.

"Lovely to see you too," Arianna replied sarcastically, as she walked right past her into the living room. She was glad she was looking semi-presentable today, wearing a peach-colored sundress with her hair up in a *chignon*. She took off her matching sandals when she noticed the beautiful plush white carpeting along with the modern, expensive-looking couch and coffee table in her living room. There was also a leather recliner which matched the carpeting and Arianna couldn't help but wonder how Esther managed to keep everything so stain-free. She was pretty much in awe, because she knew it would only take her an hour living in this place before she'd permanently stain something. Arianna noticed many gold framed pictures of Esther around the living room, where it was obvious that another person, of the male persuasion, had been cut out. Man, she certainly does exhibit traits of a serial killer, she thought. "Nice place," she remarked.

"Yeah yeah, what do you want?" Esther replied impatiently. Arianna began to develop a much deeper appreciation for the police, because of them being forced to deal with snotty suspects and perps all day long. She resolved to be a little nicer to Mike the next time she saw him.

"As I mentioned before, we're investigating Phil's death."

"Well, you were there, weren't you, you saw what I saw," she said, hands on her hips.

"Of course, but I'd like to get some background information on the deceased," she replied defensively.

She smirked. "'The deceased?' How formal for someone who was all over him on the dance floor."

Arianna lost it and began jabbing her finger at her. "Listen, lose the attitude or I will bring some men here from the department to bring you down to the station to interview you. I'm sure your friends and neighbors would love to watch that happen, wouldn't they?"

Esther shut her mouth and then politely asked, "What do you want to know?"

Arianna sat down on the recliner and pulled out her notebook. "Let's start with how long have you been attending St. Francis and how long had you known Phil?"

"I've been going there about six years and would see Phil, maybe a couple of times a year in church, but I've seen him several times at the dances. I never knew him prior to his divorce." Esther spat the last word out as if it were contagious.

"Can you think of anyone who would harbor a grudge against him?" she asked her. While she waited for Esther's response, Arianna looked around a little more. A bookcase in the hallway, containing many self-help books between two expensive-looking, white marble bookends, caught her attention. She specifically noticed two in particular, <u>Why do Men Suck?</u> and <u>How to Bleed your Ex Dry</u>, both by Dr. Sue Hymnphorallheesgott, a relatively famous German author, who'd been involved in a string of notorious divorces. It appeared as if Esther also owned her latest bestseller, <u>Getting Back at Him, Mobster Style</u>.

"Can't say that I do. Maybe you should ask his ex-wife, I'm sure she could list all of his shortcomings for you," she replied in a cocky manner.

"You know Esther, I'm beginning to think you have a big chip on your shoulder."

"Oh?" she said, actually sounding surprised.

"Well, of course. You called me a floozy, without even knowing me, just because I was dancing with Phil. We were both single and weren't doing anything inappropriate at the time. Therefore, I'd have to guess that you were perhaps, madly in love with Phil yourself and insanely jealous of me."

"Ha!" she scoffed, "madly in love with Phil? Hardly!" she said, while she avoided looking at Arianna.

"Well then, no offense, but just because your husband left you for a much younger woman, don't take your anger out on all young nubile women."

She folded her arms across her chest. "Is that all?"

Arianna looked at her directly. "You know, the medical examiner is not sure what Phil died of exactly."

"Yeah, so what?" Esther said.

"Just curious, if Phil was drugged or poisoned for some reason and you had to guess who did it, who would you suspect?"

"I really can't think of anyone, except perhaps your mother," she replied smugly.

"My mother, are you crazy?" Arianna answered, shocked.

"Hey, you asked for my opinion. I've seen your mother at St. Francis a few times eyeing up the rich guys. Who knows? Maybe he had spurned her advances and she became angry and jealous because Phil was attracted to you and not her, and offed him?" Esther suggested.

She shook her head. "Now I know you're off your rocker. I could easily see my mother nagging someone to death, but murder – no," Arianna said, slightly rattled. She hurriedly changed the subject. "Stanley mentioned you covered for him at the bar that night," she stated.

"Yes, and if you're asking if I poisoned him, the answer is no."

"How many times did you cover for Stanley?"

"Twice, I think," Esther replied.

"Do you remember what times you covered for him?"

"Heck no, is this really relevant?"

"Maybe, maybe not. Were you called away at all while tending bar?" Arianna asked her.

"No, I wasn't," she said in a tone of voice that implied she wanted this interview to be over with, as soon as possible.

"Did you notice anything suspicious at all?" Esther shook her head.

Arianna stood up. "I think that's about it then. Thank you for your time," she told her as she left Esther's condo, just as glad as Esther was, that the interview was finished.

When Arianna got home, the first thing she did was call Mike. "Get this; Esther Sullivan suggested my mom might have something to do with Phil's death!" She briefed him on their conversation.

"Ha, Sandra? Hilarious! What made Esther think that?" asked Mike.

"She implied that my mother went to the dances to snag a rich guy and that Phil probably rejected her, and so as soon as she saw him with me, she went into a jealous rage and killed him. Like seriously? I guess she figured my mother just so happened to be carrying some deadly poison, in case it came in handy someday," Arianna said sarcastically.

"Well, you should probably interview her anyway," he replied.

"What? Why?"

"When a suspect tells you that someone who was there at the time of the murder might have something to do with that murder, it's our duty to investigate it, no matter how wacky we might think it is," Mike patiently explained.

"Oh geez, how would she even get the drug or whatever into Phil's drink?" she pointedly asked him.

"It's standard police procedure, Riann. Your mother was there, after all, and another suspect mentioned her specifically, of possibly having a motive."

"Yeah, but the alleged motive was because she was jealous of me. Now, she's been disappointed in me, disgusted by me, but jealous of me? No way. Besides, I'm sure the only reason Esther accused my mother, is because she defended me when Esther called me a floozy at the dance."

"Oh c'mon Riann, it might be fun to interview Sandra," Mike tried to placate her. He smiled, imagining Sandra's almost certain negative reaction to Arianna's questioning.

"It'll be anything but fun," she said, kicking off her sandals and making her way to the refrigerator. *Crap, I'm out of wine*!

"You know, something's kind of eating at me in regards to one of the suspects," she told him.

"Oh?"

"Yeah, it's weird, one of them reminds me of Cassie Rogers, a high school classmate of mine, but the funny thing is she doesn't look anything like her at all. But when I see her, I automatically think of Cassie."

"Huh, maybe it's her facial expression?" Mike suggested.

"Yeah, maybe..."

"Isn't Cassie that whack-job you've told me about a few times? Which suspect reminds you of her?"

"Yes, that's her, but eh, it's not important, forget I said anything," she replied.

"Oh, I got that information you asked for on the Ciccone/ La Paglia family feud," Mike told her.

"Yes?" she responded, deciding to make do with a root beer.

"Here's the scoop. Evidently, many many years ago, one of the Ciccone family sons, Luigi, became embroiled in a vicious argument with an Anthony La Paglia in Sicily. They were both in their twenties and the fight was over a girl. Luigi had been fooling around with Anthony's *fiancée*. Anthony pushed Luigi hard and he fell and hit his head on a rock. Sadly, he died a few hours later. Afterwards, the two families despised each other for decades. However, many years have passed since then and according to my sources, the feud actually ended about thirty years ago. There are even two or three marriages made in recent years between the families, so it appears there's no longer a vendetta."

"Great! Another good lead shot to hell," she responded, not being able to hide the anger and frustration in her voice. "Sooo," Arianna tried to sound casual, "how was your night, last night?"

"Good, how was yours?" Mike answered.

"Mine was fine." She waited for him to mention Barbara and it began to infuriate her when he didn't. "Well, I couldn't help but notice as I was leaving, that Barbara came over last night..."

"Yes, she did."

"Well?" she asked him, feeling both annoyed and frustrated.

"Well what?"

She raised her voice, "Was there some particular reason why she came over?"

"Yes, there was," he calmly replied.

"Geez Louise Mike, are you going to make me say it? WHY DID SHE COME OVER LAST NIGHT?!"

"She came over to discuss something with me, nothing to worry your pretty little head about," he assured her.

"Uh huh," she said in an angry tone.

He challenged her, "Hey, why is it okay for you to ask me about Barbara, when I got in trouble with you for asking about your blind date the other night?"

She thought over what he said for a moment. "You're right Mike, I'm sorry. What you do with Barbara is your business. We're not officially dating or anything, and you have the right to talk to or see Barbara or any bimbo you want. You obviously don't need my permission to do so."

If Arianna thought Mike would deny there was anything physical going on with Barbara, he wasn't taking the bait. "Thank you, I appreciate that. Uh, listen Riann before I forget, I'd like to offer you a piece of advice," Mike said. Uh oh, she thought, that was always bad. Because Mike was so much older than her, he believed he was that much wiser than her, and loved nothing more than to give her unsolicited advice. Arianna would get upset afterwards, which would inevitably lead to an argument. "I would drop the notebook when interviewing suspects," he told her.

"Why?" she asked, feeling insulted.

"Because you don't notice as many details during the interview, like the nuances in their voice, body language, etc., when you're busy writing," Mike explained.

"I understand that, but how do you propose I remember everything they say then, without writing it down?" she responded, growing defensive.

"Just write all of it down afterwards, when you're in the car," he told her.

Arianna whined, "I'm not going to be able to remember what was said, if I have to wait until I'm in the car."

"You were a waitress, Riann. I don't understand how you could have such a horrible memory."

"Arrgh!" she yelled in the phone, ending the call abruptly. She scrounged around in her purse for her keys. It was time to go for a liquor run.

Chapter Eleven - A Horrific Day

Early in the afternoon the next day, Arianna made herself a huge hamburger from some ground beef she had left over in her freezer. Luckily, there was just barely enough mustard and ketchup in the refrigerator, for one burger. Arianna despised shopping, and as a consequence, quite often ran out of things. After lunch, she spent time curled up with Tony and Carmela, finally starting a book her sister gave her last year, How to Snag a Man without Appearing Desperate. After about a half hour, she closed the book. *This has got to be the most stupid book I have ever read,* she thought.

A few hours later, Arianna was checking her email in-box on her laptop, when a notice from a local bookstore, forwarded by her mother caught her eye. She clicked on it and read, "Your order of Beggars Can't Be Choosers, a Guide for Single Women in Their Thirties, will be ready for pick up tomorrow. Have a nice day!" She gave a deep long sigh. *Why oh why, couldn't she have just been given a normal family, one who wasn't so meddlesome and annoying?*

Her cell phone began vibrating on the coffee table. It was Sallie Rigelli. She picked up immediately. "Hi Sallie."

"Hi Riann, I'm calling because I think there's something you should know," she said.

"Oh?" Arianna replied, curious.

"You are never going to believe this," Sallie blurted out excitedly, "but Stanley was Phil's biological father!"

"Phil's father?" That was definitely not what she was expecting; Arianna could hardly believe her ears. She quickly found a chair. *I need to be sitting for this.*

"Stanley never told anyone about it. He thought it was better to just keep it a secret, so nobody knew, not even Phil. Phil's mother, Carol came to see Stanley about ten years ago, right before she died, and told him that Phil was his. She and Stanley had a brief affair many years ago. Her husband of course, assumed he was Phil's father, and Carol never led him to believe otherwise. Stanley has never married and he never had any other children. From what Stanley's told me, he was quite the ladies' man back in the day. Of course, that's no surprise considering how awesome he..."

"When did you find this out?" Arianna interrupted her, excitement in her voice.

"Just yesterday. I felt so honored that he would share his secret with me. Can you imagine Riann, if Phil would have lived and you two got married, and Stanley and I got married, I would have been your mother-in-law!"

"I'm sorry, I don't want a mother-in-law who's younger than me and looks better than I do," Arianna quickly replied. "Now, if my TV show knowledge serves me correctly, the fact that Stanley is Phil's father, should not affect Paula La Paglia's inheritance whatsoever. Since he died intestate, or without a will, everything goes to the next of kin, which does not include parents." She paused for a moment. "Listen, Sallie, thank you so much for telling me. I don't know if it will have any bearing on this case or not, but it's definitely a very interesting development."

"I thought it would be," Sallie replied proudly.

"Hey Sallie, I don't feel like I'm getting very far in this investigation. Since we seemed to work well together last year during all the St. James hoopla, do you think you could help me out a little? In your free time, of course. You know, maybe you could come on some interviews with me; I think your intuition might come in handy."

Sallie screamed into the phone. "Yes, of course, Riann! Oh this is going to be sooo exciting and awesome!"

After pulling the phone away from her ear, she replied, "Just so you understand though, I'll be asking all the questions, okay?"

"Oh, that's fine. You'll be Dr. House and I'll be your Dr. Wilson, and you can use me to bounce ideas off of!" Dr. House and Dr. Wilson were characters in a TV show called House that both women watched religiously.

"Yeah, something like that, although it's not really a fair comparison, because House is pretty nasty to Wilson." Arianna frowned, noticing that Sallie didn't immediately jump in and agree with her. She spent the next twenty minutes; however, filling Sallie in on the investigation.

"So, is there anything I should be doing right now?" Sallie asked.

"No, not yet, just keep your eyes and ears open. I'll call you when I need you."

"Alright, well have a good," she paused, "oh I almost forgot Riann, I had a premonition when I woke up this morning."

"Oh no, is there going to be another death?" Arianna worriedly exclaimed.

"No, I just want you to be careful. I feel there's a cloud over you today. Oh, hold on a minute," Sallie said, distracted. She put her hand over the receiver. "Stanley, don't eat that! I need to cut your steak for you first; you don't have your teeth in. Sorry Riann, but I've got to go."

"Oh, OK, well thanks for the warning, and also for agreeing to help me with the investigation. Have a good one," she told her in a shaky voice, betraying her worry.

"You too," Sallie replied and hung up.

A couple of hours later, Arianna had already forgotten about the dire prediction and decided to go sit out on her front porch, and enjoy the really beautiful Chicago spring day. There were two white wicker chairs with peacock blue cushions on her spacious front porch and a white porch swing that she liked to rock in from time to time.

Arianna sat in the swing thinking about the fact that she'd have to eventually interrogate her mother, when all of a sudden, she heard a man yelling, "Please calm down and come back inside!"

"No, you are such an asshole! I can't believe I was stupid enough to marry you!"

Arianna froze and stopped rocking. *Geez, that's Susie fighting with her husband. Wonderful, I assumed when we were both laid off, that I had finally escaped from hearing all about her personal life.*

Susie, Arianna's ex-co-worker, drove her crazy. She never shut up and always revealed EVERYTHING to EVERYBODY about her personal life. There were no boundaries with her at all; thereby, rendering her the exact opposite of Arianna, who very much loved and appreciated boundaries. As a rule, she tried to avoid Susie as much as possible; however, to Arianna's horror this past year, they had become neighbors.

"No, I'm not going to calm down, go to Hell!" A short and stocky woman in her forties, with medium-length, black curly hair, brown eyes, and an olive complexion, stalked off and noticed Arianna sitting on her porch. Before she had a chance to hide, Susie asked with a tear-stained face, "Riann, can I please stay with you for a few days?"

"A few days...," Arianna echoed, trying to come up with any polite excuse. Of course, as always, under tremendous pressure, her mind drew a blank. "Umm, why?" she asked her, awkwardly pretending that she hadn't overheard their extremely loud argument.

"I think Carl is having an affair!" she blurted out.

"Really, how terrible!" Arianna said. *What took him so long?*

"I just can't be with him, or even look at him right now, and I can't afford a motel," explained Susie.

"Uh, why don't you just kick him out?" Arianna helpfully suggested. "He's the jerk who cheated on you, remember. Why should I, I mean you, be inconvenienced?"

"Carl will never leave the house. Please Riann, I swear, I'll stay out of your way."

"Sure," she replied, her face solemn, shoulders slumped, now resembling a death-row prisoner doomed to her fate.

"Great! I'll go pack a few things and will be over in a half an hour," she said cheerily.

Arianna nodded, as Susie ran home. She got up and stood gravely on her front porch, looking up at the sky and asking plaintively, "Really God, really? What did I ever do to you, except you know, be so sinful you had to sacrifice your only son and all?" She walked back inside her house, severely depressed.

About forty minutes later, Susie came back with a giant suitcase and pillow.

"You're just staying a couple of nights, right?" Arianna asked fearfully, holding the front door open for her.

"Oh yes, of course. I just brought everything I thought I might need and then some, because I don't want to have to go back into that house."

"OK," Arianna sighed, and walked her through her home. She pointed to a small room off to the side of the dining room, "That's the guest bedroom over there."

"Wonderful, I'll just unpack my stuff," Susie said, heading towards it, as the cats ran and hid under the coffee table.

Arianna realized that another one of Susie's horrible predictions had come true. She walked into the kitchen and pulled out a bottle of *Moscato d'Asti* from the fridge. *It's going to be a long night. Thank God, I had the presence of mind to make a liquor run yesterday.* She decided she would lock herself in her room with the bottle and go over her notes from the case. After about fifteen minutes, she could hear the sounds of loud sobbing coming from the guest room. Arianna easily made the decision to ignore it. A few minutes later, the sobbing turned into loud moaning and wailing. Dammit, she thought, now I'm going to have to go in and check on her. She groaned, jumped off her bed, walked over to Susie's room and knocked on the door.

"Hello? Susie uh, I'm just making sure everything's okay," Arianna said, trying to sound concerned, but not too concerned, not concerned enough to make Susie feel she could confide in her. "You don't have to open the door or anything...," she was saying, when the door suddenly sprang open.

"Oh Riann!" She grabbed and hugged her. "I feel so alone!" she wailed. Arianna was in utter agony. She didn't care for public displays of affection, or private ones either for that matter, unless it was from someone she was dating, of course. She felt extremely awkward, and considering the fact that it was Susie who was presently squeezing the life out of her, the uncomfortableness she was experiencing, was multiplied to the third power. "What am I going to do?" she buried her head in Arianna's chest, as Susie was about seven inches shorter than her.

"Oh geez, oh God," she said, patting her head awkwardly, not knowing what to do with her hands. "Everything is going to be fine."

"But how do you know that?" she mumbled.

Arianna sighed. "I just do." Susie finally raised her head up off her chest and Arianna noticed her nose was running. Consequently, she was trying not to think about all the snot that was probably left all over her shirt. Susie had calmed down a bit, so she took the advantage of the opportunity to leave. "OK, well, I'm going to go back to my room now, I'm a little tired," she said, as she slowly backed out of the guest bedroom.

"Oh, OK," Susie replied, sniffling.

Arianna returned to her room and called Mike at home to inform him of the latest unfortunate turn of events. He had told her he was off this evening, but the phone just rang and rang, and the machine (Mike was old school and still preferred an answering machine over voice mail) never picked up. Arianna was a little worried because she knew this only happened when Mike turned the ringer off at home during those times when he didn't want to be disturbed. *Hmmm, that's strange.* She decided not to think about it, she had enough catastrophes to deal with at the moment.

Even though it was a warm spring day in Chicagoland, she changed into her white flannel, long-sleeved granny nightgown, which literally covered every inch of her body. Again, she had forgotten to do the laundry and it was the only thing available for her to wear to bed, besides going *au naturel*. Of course, if you knew Arianna, you'd know that was NOT going to happen. She turned her ceiling fan on high and nestled in for what she hoped would be a good night's sleep.

Twenty minutes later, when she was just about to drift off into welcome slumber, she heard loud noises like things getting slammed around, coming from Susie's room. "Oh Jesus!" she said aloud, as she jumped out of bed again and went to see what was going on. She stuck her head in the doorway and saw Susie muttering loudly to herself, and whipping her belongings around the bedroom.

"Hey, what's going on here?" Arianna asked Susie, who was completely freaking out.

"I am just so furious at Carl! You know, I could have had an affair too. That guy Angelo who works at the Italian deli, you should see the way he looks at me, I tell you. And if this bimbo wants him, I say fine, he's not even that great in bed! Half the time, he just collapses on top of me and…"

At this point, Arianna stuck her fingers in her ears, and began singing, "la la la la la la la, I can't hear you." Unfortunately, Susie did not catch the blatant hint and kept talking anyway. That night, long after the two women went to bed, Arianna was awakened several times by Susie's sniffling and muffled sobs. Needless to say, she did not get much sleep and was even crankier than usual the next morning.

Around 10:00 am, Mike Stevenson, in full police attire, rang Arianna's doorbell. He immediately recognized the woman who answered the door, her face full of anguish.

"Oh, hello Susie," he said, sounding surprised, "is Riann around?"

"Yes, but she's in bed right now," said Susie, wearing a grey sweatshirt with matching sweatpants, and looking much more somber than Mike had ever seen her before.

"In bed?" he asked worriedly, "did something happen to her?"

"Oh no," Susie reassured him, "first thing this morning, Riann told me she had a raging headache, and that she was going back to bed. She said she was not to be disturbed the entire day, no matter what."

"I see," Mike replied, somewhat relieved. "Do you mind if I ask what you're doing here?"

To Mike's consternation, she began crying hysterically. "Carl, my husband, is a big womanizing philanderer!"

She went on for a couple of minutes, telling him how stupid she had been for the last twenty-five years. After a while even he, a seasoned veteran of dealing with Arianna's histrionics, couldn't take it anymore and cut her off. "I need to see Riann," he told her authoritatively.

"Oh? Are you two dating again?" she asked curiously.

"No," he paused, "I'm on official police business."

"Well in that case, go ahead." She stepped out of his way and hollered in a loud, whiny, grating voice, (Arianna always likened it to Howard Wolowitz's mother's voice on the TV series, <u>The Big Bang Theory</u>). "Riann, Mike Stevenson is here on official police business!" When there was no response, she loudly whispered, "Maybe she's asleep?"

Mike nodded at her and said, "I'll check and see."

He knocked lightly on her bedroom door. An exasperated voice rang out, "Susie, I told you I can't be disturbed, I'm extremely ill!"

Mike walked into her room. "It's me, you nincompoop. Susie filled me in, and I'm guessing this illness is an elaborate sham to avoid her?"

"Bingo, you win the prize," Arianna replied sarcastically. She was lying on her back on top of the bed, massaging her temples with both hands. "Although, now I really do have a headache. If I hear one more time about how horrible Carl is in the sack, I'm going to go insane."

"Well," Mike said, smiling, "I have good news for you then, I'm going to rescue you."

"Oh?" she said, sitting up, "tell me more."

"First, I have to ask, what the hell are you wearing? What's with the *burka*?"

"Oh," she said dismissively, "my mom gave it to me as a gift a few years back, but I never got a chance to wear it, so I thought I'd put it on last night."

He looked at her with skeptical eyes. "You just forgot to do laundry again, didn't you?"

She guiltily looked down at the floor. "Maybe...," she answered.

"Riann, how could you forget to do laundry all the time, I don't understand..."

"Stop," she cut him off, "you were about to tell me why you're here, not judge me on my domestic skills."

"Anyway, I came to take you to breakfast."

"Really?" she asked suspiciously. "Why?"

"Because I'm in a generous mood." Arianna just stared at him skeptically. "Alright, I just wanted to apologize for trying to tell you how you should handle the suspect interviews."

"Well, since I'm hungry and have a hankering for Eggs Benedict, I'll accept your apology. Let me get dressed." She briskly shooed him out of her bedroom.

Arianna pulled on a pair of denim shorts with a stretchy elastic waistband, a tight black T-shirt that in silver letters said, "Too Hot to Handle", and slid her feet into an old pair of brown sandals. When she came out of her room, Susie saw her and said, "Oh good, you're feeling better, I..."

Mike interrupted her, "Please excuse us Susie, I have to bring Riann to the station right away. There are some new developments in an investigation that she's helping us with." Before she could reply, the two swiftly ran out the door and into the squad car, leaving Susie standing there, looking forlornly out the window.

"That was brilliant!" Arianna said, looking over at him while he started up the car.

"It was, wasn't it," he chuckled, as he pulled out of her driveway.

Mike drove her to Patty's Pancake House, their favorite breakfast place, just a few minutes away. After they sat down and were served their coffee and Eggs Benedicts, Arianna spoke first, "Just so you know, I've asked Sallie Rigelli to help me out with this case."

"Whaa?" Mike replied and started choking. After a minute of coughing, he looked at her and said, "Well, whatever you think is best. If you think a twenty-something girl, who dresses like a bimbo and is dating a man older than God, could be of any help to you, then by all means rely on Sallie."

Arianna glared at him. "You forget about her Gift!"

He glared back at her. "Don't even go there, Riann, I'm not going to get into that same old argument again with you."

She tried reasoning with him. "Sallie won't be asking any questions or anything. She'll be my Dr. Wilson, I'll just bounce ideas off of her."

"Doctor who? Oh never mind, do you not see that Sallie is dating a suspect in a murder investigation? There's a total conflict of interest there." He paused for a minute, then added, "Well, if he is the killer, he'll be dead by the time the case goes to trial anyway, so I guess you can go ahead and include Sallie in on what you're doing."

She smiled. "Thank you! I knew you'd understand."

Mike groaned, "OK, I have to ask though, besides her alleged 'Gift', why exactly did you ask Sallie to help you with this case?"

"I thought we made a pretty good team last year when I solved the two murders at the church. Remember, I wouldn't have even started investigating, if it wasn't for Sallie. She was instrumental to the investigation that brought a killer to justice. Besides," she said, blushing a little, "it was kind of fun pairing up with her at the time."

Mike said resignedly, "Alright fine. Truce?" He stuck his hand out.

"Truce," she agreed and shook it firmly.

"Riann, I do have some new information for you. We finally received access from the phone company to Phil's call records, and the only person he contacted the day he died was his daughter Paula, late that morning."

"Interesting," she replied, with her mouth half full, savoring her Canadian bacon.

"We also got a look at his GPS. It turns out he visited Sarah Brewster in the early afternoon for about forty-five minutes, then he went home. In the late afternoon, he left his house to go to Rachel Gordon's for about twenty-five minutes, and then returned home. The last time he went out, was that evening to St. Francis Church, and as you know, he never returned."

"What time did Phil arrive at the dance?" she asked.

"Around 7:30 pm," he replied.

"My mom and I got there around 7:45 pm I think, so he really wasn't there very long before we arrived."

"That's right, and he didn't start experiencing symptoms, according to you and others at the dance, until around 9:15 pm. There was no food or drink found in his vehicle. Since we don't know for certain that Phil was poisoned at the dance, it's important that we know why he made those visits."

"I'm on it, like wild on rice," she replied enthusiastically.

"Riann, it's 'white' on rice, not 'wild'," Mike pointed out, laughing.

"Whatever," she replied, imperturbed, "it seems I'm going to have to talk to all three of these women again. I'll call Sallie and fill her in later."

They enjoyed the rest of their breakfast together munching in silence and were back in the car, when Arianna turned to Mike and asked, "So, how's Barbara doing?" She said the word Barbara, the way a Jew would say the name Hitler.

"She's fine," he replied, close lipped as usual.

"Hmmph," she said in response, turning her back on him and looking out her window.

When Mike dropped her off at home afterwards, Arianna ran directly over to Carl and Susie's house, an average-sized, red brick home with a yellow awning. There were red tulips planted all around the front yard and what appeared to be a huge junkyard in the back. Their backyard was filled with old tires lying about, old motorcycle parts strewn all over, tons of shoes, sports equipment, and too many other eyesores to list. She knocked on their front door.

Carl, about 5'8", bald, and fat, bordering on obese, answered the door. He was wearing faded blue jeans and a stained white undershirt filled with holes that revealed an unseemly amount of light-brown armpit hair. "Yeah?"

Wow, what a prize. I can see why Susie's so broken up over him. "I'm your neighbor Arianna, Susie is staying with me."

"Yeah, I know," he said grumpily.

"I want you two to make up," she told him bluntly.

"I didn't even do anything wrong! I just had a long-distance flirtation on the Internet. I was bored and curious one day, so I went on LustMatch and…"

"Stop! I don't care what you did or didn't do. Either make up with your wife today, or I'll talk to my boyfriend, the Chief of the Meadowville Police Department, about all the code violations you have in your backyard."

With an alarmed look on his face, he muttered, "Alright, I'll see what I can do."

Arianna left, and instead of entering her house through the front door, she walked around the house and went in through her back door instead. She ran downstairs into the basement and started a load of laundry. Arianna entered her basement only when she was forced to do laundry, on account of all the millipedes she'd spotted over the years. As a precaution, she always made sure she wore shoes, and, if she was feeling extra nervous, winter boots.

A half hour later, Susie cheerfully ran down the stairs into the basement. "Guess what Riann?!"

"I have no idea," Arianna replied, pulling clothes out of the washer.

"Carl and I made up!" Susie beamed.

"Really? How wonderful." She tried to look surprised.

"Yes, he didn't actually have an affair, he…"

Arianna stopped her in mid-sentence. "I don't need to know the details, just as long as you two lovebirds are back together. Let's just get you packed, shall we?" She ran upstairs and started throwing Susie's things back into her suitcase.

After Susie left and, from Arianna's point-of-view, all was right with the world again, she called Sallie and told her the latest news from Mike. They both agreed that Arianna would interview Sandra by phone, and then she would come around and pick Sallie up. They would go and visit Rachel Gordon first.

Chapter Twelve - Interesting Developments

Arianna took a deep breath and mustered up the gumption to call her mother. "Hey Mom, how are you?" she asked in a fake cheerful voice.

"I'm fine Arianna, why are you so mean to your sister?"

"She told you I was being mean to her?" she asked incredulously.

Sandra admonished her, "Just because the man does not have a television addiction problem like you, doesn't mean you should drop him like a hot potato."

"Television addiction?" Arianna's temper flared up, her face grew flushed, and she began throwing her arms in the air. "The man didn't even OWN a TV, and he had absolutely no personality to speak of!"

"Arianna, you are much too picky. Now did you call me just to argue, or is there supposed to be a point to this conversation?"

"Fine, let's drop the subject, that is not why I called," she replied, testily.

"Well?" her mother asked impatiently.

"The reports came back inconclusive as to the cause of Phil La Paglia's death. Mike's boss, the Superintendent, asked Mike to hire me as a consultant in the investigation into his death, because of my success with the St. James murders, so…"

Her mother interrupted her, "Oh that was such a tedious and depressing business." She gave a great sigh.

"Mom, I solved two murders there, almost singlehandedly."

"I know, but seriously Arianna, can't you do something that won't put you in the spotlight so much? It is a little tacky, you know." She added, "Besides, what man would want to marry a nosy detective?"

Arianna made a face and continued, "So, as I was saying before I was so rudely interrupted, since I'm helping out with the investigation, I need to ask you some questions about Phil and a few of the ladies at the Singles Dance.

"But why are you questioning me? Mike had already asked me if I noticed anything unusual and I said no."

"Oh you know, I thought you might have some helpful insights," Arianna said.

"Really? But I hardly know any of them at all," she said with a suspicious tone to her voice.

"Still, I'd like to get your point of view," insisted Arianna.

"Arianna, what is going on? I always know when you're holding back on me," she told her.

Damn, she thought, how do mothers do that? "Mom please, just help me out here. Had you ever seen Phil before? Had you ever spoken to him?"

"I'd seen him before, but I had never spoken to him, why would I? I don't go around talking to strange men I've never met, you know," she answered.

"Why haven't you ever talked to Phil? He was a good-looking man, I would've thought you might have been attracted to him."

"Oh please Arianna, he never approached me and a lady never makes the first move, didn't I teach you ANYTHING?" she asked reproachfully.

Arianna took a deep breath and with great effort managed to control herself, mainly so she wouldn't have to hear a lecture from her mother on how her hotheadedness turns off men. "Well, can you tell me what you do know about him? Mom, this is serious, I need all the help I can get."

"I'm sorry Arianna, I'll try my best to help you, but I'm afraid I don't know much. As you know, I disdain gossip as a rule and I've only seen him at three or four dances. I haven't been coming to these dances that long, only in the past year and a half or so, and they're only once a month. I had seen a flyer posted at the library about St. Francis Church events and they looked like they might be fun, so I decided to give it a go. I do know that Phil always drank JB and water, because I've been close enough to hear his bar order a few times."

"Did you ever overhear Phil talking about having an argument or fight with anyone, or did you ever hear anybody discussing Phil at all?"

"No, not that I can recall," she replied.

"Alright, what can you tell me about Sarah and the ladies, Rachel, Esther, and Camille?" Arianna, contrary to Mike's suggestions, was quickly jotting everything down in her notebook.

"I've talked to Sarah a few times, she seems like she has a good head on her shoulders. Rachel, I've never talked to, nor have I ever heard her say anything, she's pretty soft spoken. Camille is very odd and never looks happy and Esther, well, she can be quite nasty, as you witnessed. She hates her ex-husband with a passion. Now if he had dropped dead and not Phil, I would say there'd be no doubt in anybody's mind that she was the killer."

"Yes, well thanks again for sticking up for me Mom," she said.

"What are mothers for, dear?"

"Last question, I know Mike already asked you this, but please think hard before you answer, you might remember something you've forgotten. Did you notice anything out of the ordinary that night?" she asked.

She paused for a few seconds. "Nothing strange, except maybe that Stanley was making more trips to the bathroom than usual."

Again, Stanley and his bathroom trips, ugh. Arianna's stomach turned, because any mention of Stanley now conjured up extremely gross pictures in her head. "That's it Mom, thanks for your help, I'll let you go."

"Have a good day," her mother replied.

As soon as the call ended with her mother, Arianna phoned Sallie. After two and a half rings, Sallie picked up the call. "I'm coming over in five minutes," Arianna told her.

She drove over to her condo, which was located on the outskirts of Meadowville. Sallie was waiting outside for her in such an outrageous outfit, that even by Sallie Rigelli standards, it would be considered extreme. She happened to be dressed exactly like "Elvira, Mistress of the Dark", the old horror TV host, wearing a long, EXTREMELY low-cut black dress, which was originally intended to be a "sexy witch" Halloween costume/lingerie. She was also sporting very long, fake red fingernails to boot. "Wow!" Arianna said, as she got in the car.

"What?" Sallie asked, inspecting her fingernails, oblivious to the impact her outfit had made.

"Nothing," she replied, and shook her head. They made their way over to Rachel Gordon's house, and coincidentally, just as they parked their car, Rachel pulled up in a little blue Volkswagen.

"Perfect timing, it seems," Arianna said triumphantly. Rachel got out of her car carrying a bag of groceries from Trader Joes, as if it were a giant boulder.

"Aww, what a cute little lady, she kind of reminds me of my grandmother," Sallie said in a syrupy-sweet voice.

Arianna responded by, evidently, channeling Mike Stevenson. "You have to focus Sallie, and leave your personal feelings out of it.

She could be a murderer, you know." Sallie nodded, slightly embarrassed.

Arianna waved and walked quickly over to Rachel, slyly peeked inside her bag and saw one gallon of iced tea, one bottle of Vitamin C and a giant chocolate bar. "Here, let me help you with that," Arianna offered, taking the bag from her.

As they walked up the front steps together, Rachel appeared bewildered and mildly annoyed. "I'm sorry, why are you both here?" she asked, staring at Sallie's outfit.

"Oh yes," Arianna set the bag down on Rachel's porch. "This is my friend and associate, Sallie Rigelli." Rachel continued to look at Sallie as if she had three heads. "The police examined the GPS navigating system on Phil's car, and it appears as if the last place he went to the day he died, was yours at 3:30 pm."

"Yes? Is there a question you have?" Rachel asked in response.

"Tell us about that visit. The GPS tells us that he stayed at your house for about twenty-five minutes and then went home."

"He came over to drop off a check," she replied defensively.

"And that took twenty-five minutes?" asked Arianna.

"Well, no. We chit-chatted a little bit."

"What did you talk about?"

"Nothing in particular."

"Did he eat or drink anything while he was here?"

"Uh yes I think so," she looked as if she was in deep thought. "Yes, I I gave him water," she stammered.

"Thank you for helping us Rachel," Arianna replied.

Looking unsure of herself, she hesitatingly asked, "Would you two like some coffee and pie?"

Sallie adjusted her cleavage and looked at Arianna for a cue. "No thank you, we'd love to, but we have a lot of things to get done today," Arianna said sincerely. "Maybe we can take a rain check?"

Rachel nodded and turned towards her front door as the two women took their leave.

Once they were safely out of earshot, Arianna asked, "OK, what did you pick up in there?"

"Just the fact that she's very sad and lonely," Sallie said.

"Yeah, I can see that being true, but I don't think that really helps us much. Killers can be sad and lonely too, you know," said Arianna.

"Well sorry, but The Gift doesn't work like that, I can't just direct it to tell me if a person is a murderer or not. There are some things we're just not meant to know, I guess," she said, clearly a little irritated.

"I understand, I'm sorry. I'm just frustrated, I so very much want to solve this case."

"Don't worry, Riann. I have total faith in you!" Sallie told her, giving her a side hug.

"Thanks Sallie, I really do appreciate it," replied Arianna, already feeling better.

Next, they drove to Paula La Paglia's house, and as the two women approached the front door, Arianna cautioned Sallie, "Don't sit down or touch anything, if you can avoid it." Sallie looked at her with a puzzled expression. "I don't want you to catch anything while you're helping me out on this case," she explained, and rang the doorbell. The door opened suddenly, catching them both off guard.

"Oh, it's you," Paula flatly stated.

"Yes, I have a couple more questions for you. This is my associate, Sallie Rigelli, may we come in?"

Evidently not noticing or caring about Sallie's attire, she glumly replied, "I suppose so," and turned her back on them. She returned to her sofa and continued watching the Weather Channel on TV, ignoring the two women. The place looked exactly the same as it did the last time Arianna visited, although the stench had dissipated a little. She must have changed the litter box for the month, Arianna thought to herself. *I bet you anything this chick is a hoarder.* Hoarders was another one of Arianna's favorite TV shows. She'd get so mad at the hoarder; however, that inevitably, she'd start screaming obscenities at the television set. "When you start misplacing your pets AND your grandchildren due to your disgusting mess, it's time to admit you have a problem!" was her final opinion on the matter. She would work herself up into such frenzy, that she'd even make Mike, a seasoned cop, nervous and so he refused to watch the show with her anymore.

"The police had retrieved Phil's phone records from the day he died and evidently, he called you at 2:00 pm, and you talked for a half an hour. Do you recall what that conversation was about?" Arianna questioned her.

"Yes," she answered sullenly, turning her attention back to the TV.

Arianna waited, then said, "Well?"

"Well what?" Paula replied.

"Well, what did you talk about?" she asked, annoyed.

"And why exactly do you need to know that?"

"Paula, I'm not here to answer your questions, I'm here to have my questions answered. We want to know what your father was doing, where he was going, who he was talking to, EVERYTHING that happened that day. Not only because it may lead us to know how and when a drug or poison might have been administered to him, but who specifically had the motive and opportunity to do it."

"Well, if you're asking me if he told me about anyone who might want to kill him that day, the answer is no. Our discussion was all about me, like every conversation we ever had."

"Oh?" Arianna looked over at Sallie, who wasn't paying attention to their conversation at all, but appeared to be transfixed by the horrific state of Paula's living room.

"Yes, like why am I wasting my life, don't I want to get married and have children one day? Yada, yada, yada," she said.

"So you had a fight?" she asked.

"No, just our usual monthly father daughter disagreement, that's all."

"Paula," Arianna asked, "did your dad mention anyone who he was planning on meeting that day or maybe someone coming over to his house at all?"

"No," Paula replied.

"Well, I think that's all the questions we have, thank you. C'mon Sallie, let's go," she said, pulling her by the arm out of Paula's house.

When they got back in the car, Sallie told her, "Now I understand why you told me not to sit down, that place was nasty!"

"I know," Arianna agreed. "I could tell you were pretty grossed out, you seemed very distracted. Did you happen to pick up any special psychic vibes on Paula in there?"

Sallie replied, "No, I didn't pick up on anything at all, which is very weird."

"Hey, maybe extreme filthiness blocks your psychic abilities," Arianna reasoned.

"Hmm, I never heard of that," Sallie said, considering the idea, "but maybe."

"Well, perhaps we'll have better luck at Sarah's," she said optimistically.

"By the way, did you see what she was wearing?" asked Sallie. "The hideous stained smock over that blouse did not flatter her figure at ..."

Arianna interrupted her, "I get the point, she'd never win Fashionista of the year. Let's go see Sarah now."

"Alright, I hope her place isn't disgusting," said Sallie. Arianna reassured her that it wasn't.

The two women found Sarah in her front yard, pulling up weeds in her garden. "Hello again Sarah!" Arianna called out to her, "this is Sallie Rigelli, she's helping me with the investigation."

Sarah stood up, took off her gloves and looked Sallie up and down with a disapproving look on her face. "Aren't you the one dating Stanley Carter?"

"Yes, I'm his girl," she blushed.

"Isn't he a little old for you, sweetheart?"

Sallie began to launch into her, "but he's so good in bed...," explanation, so Arianna cut her off before Sallie nauseated their suspect.

"Sarah, why didn't you tell us Phil was here the day of his death?"

She seemed a little taken aback. "Well, because he was here to consult with me on a private matter, and I didn't think it was of any importance," she explained.

"Why don't you let us be the judge of that," Arianna admonished her. "What did you two discuss?"

Sarah looked annoyed. "Phil said there was a person in his life that he was beginning to feel uncomfortable around."

"Uncomfortable how?" Arianna's antennas went up.

"He wouldn't say," replied Sarah.

"Do you know if it was a man or a woman?"

"He also wouldn't say. He was extremely careful about revealing their identity and chose his words very deliberately."

"OK, what else did he say?" Arianna asked with escalating excitement, quickly pulling out her notebook and pen.

"He said he wanted to cut this person out of his life completely, but wished to do it in a respectful way that wouldn't hurt their feelings. Phil was always very considerate of other people's feelings," she, appearing a little sad, explained to them.

Arianna, clearly agitated, asked, "I still don't understand why you didn't mention all of this before?"

"Well, I didn't think it was relevant," she answered defensively.

Arianna began to lose her temper. "What? Seriously? The same day Phil was murdered, he tells you that he's having problems with someone and you DON'T think it's relevant? Are you crazy?"

Sallie gave Arianna an embarrassed look and whispered, "Riann, please."

Arianna tried to calm down. "Alright, never mind that, why was Phil telling you, specifically, all of this?"

"He said he wanted my advice, so I told him to be honest with the person. Phil told me that he was and had thought he had taken care of the matter, but was sensing that this person was not handling it very well, and he was concerned. I said, I didn't know what to tell him, because I really needed to know some specifics in order to be of any help. He told me that was okay, and that he understood, and it made him feel better just talking to me. I do seem to have that effect on people you know, for some reason they love to confide in me," Sarah told them.

"One more question, did you serve Phil any food or drink that day?"

"No," she curtly answered.

Arianna was itching to get out of there so she could discuss the latest development with Sallie. "Alright, thanks for filling us in, have a good one. Let's go Sallie," she said, motioning to her, and the two women took their leave. When they reached her car, Arianna exclaimed, "Wow, this is a MAJOR development, I can't wait to tell Mike! Phil could have been referring to the dissolution of a friendship, a work relationship, a family tie, or even a romance!"

Sallie questioned her. "I thought you said that Phil hadn't dated anyone in a long time?"

"Well, that's what people told me, but who knows? Maybe it was a secret love affair, like with a married woman or something, and that's why he was so secretive with Sarah. Regardless, it does show there was someone who was making Phil very uncomfortable and this person could very well be the murderer."

Sallie thought for a moment, and then remarked, "Unless, Sarah's making the whole thing up to draw suspicion away from herself."

"Good point Sallie!" Arianna looked at her admiringly. This was one of those times that Arianna suspected Sallie was a lot smarter than most people gave her credit for.

"I almost forgot, did you pick up anything psychic-wise on Sarah?" Arianna asked eagerly.

Appearing uneasy, Sallie responded, "Uhh..."

"C'mon, you can tell me, what is it? Is she into something really scandalous?"

"Nooo, it actually concerns you," Sallie told her.

"Me? Well, then tell me! It's alright, I'm not going to get upset," she promised her.

"OK, when you were talking with her, I just felt this negative energy shooting from her third chakra towards you. I guess I was picking up on the fact that she, well let's put it this way, you're not one of her favorite people right now."

"Ha!" Arianna folded her arms across her chest. "Well, she can join the club then, although I'm sure the 'I Despise Arianna' club has got be maxed out at full capacity by now. Although," she thought about it for a moment, "maybe she dislikes me because I'm getting close to the truth and she IS the killer! Hey, what's a third chakra anyway?"

"It's your solar plexus chakra and the center of your personal power," said Sallie. "Each of us have seven chakras in our body, they're kind of like wheels of energy."

"How does your "Gift" actually work? Do you see or hear things? Does a mysterious voice talk to you?" Arianna asked curiously.

Sallie explained, "It can come in a bunch of different ways. Sometimes, words just pop into my head. Other times, if something bad is going to happen to them soon, in my mind's eye, I'll see blackness or grayness around a person. Often, I'll just get a physical reaction, like a stomachache, which I know is telling me not to trust a person."

"You're so lucky to have that kind of gift. I wish I had something like that, which could tell me when my mom is planning on calling or coming over," Arianna said wistfully.

"You know, my third eye chakra happens to be more developed than most people, but everyone is psychic to some extent. You have psychic abilities too, you're just not conscious of them."

"Yeah, I get it," she replied, not really understanding, but too embarrassed to say so.

"And believe me, it's not all that great. A lot of times it's not very fun to sense what's about to happen, especially when people don't believe you. Also, it doesn't work very well when it comes to knowing what's going to happen to me. Remember last year, I never even saw his death coming," Sallie ruefully reminded her.

"Yeah, that's right," Arianna responded. The two women got into the car, each of them remembering last year's tragedy at St. James Christian Church, and then shared a moment of silence.

Chapter Thirteen - Stakeout

The next morning, Arianna got up early and called Mike to discuss the conversations she had with Rachel, Paula and Sarah. She was greatly encouraged when he seemed as excited as she was about Sarah's revelations. Mike told her the latest news from his end. "Riann, the medical examiner has just released the body to the family. I checked with him and there were no puncture wounds or any other holes that would indicate a bite or," he coughed delicately, "a poisoned dart. The autopsy report cites 'death by unknown causes'."

Well, that theory just blew up in my face. Arianna was just about to make a point when Mike said, "Hang on, I'm getting another call." After three minutes had passed, he got back on the line. "Sorry about that, but I have to go," he told her in a business-like voice.

"But Mike...," she started to say, when she heard a click. Arianna was left looking at her cell phone incredulously, not believing that he had just hung up on her. She frowned and walked from her living room over to the kitchen. She opened her freezer, hoping to find at least, the last remnants of what used to be a pint of cookie dough ice cream. No such luck, she discovered. *Dammit! I bet Susie ate it.*

Arianna decided she'd give Sallie a call, and try and turn her own thoughts back to the investigation. She picked up on the first ring. "Hey Sallie, why don't you come over, I have an idea."

"Sure, give me a half an hour," she said, and hung up. Within the hour, Sallie was knocking on Arianna's door. She was dressed a little more conservatively than usual in a tight red t-shirt with a silver sequined star on it and skin-tight blue jeans. Arianna figured she must have caught some flak from somebody about her Elvira outfit.

"Thanks for coming," Arianna greeted her, wearing the baggiest, most comfortable pair of white sweatpants she had and an old bleach-stained "FBI" T-shirt, which she had bought several years ago from a souvenir shop in Washington D.C. Arianna had recently come to terms with the fact that she could never compete with Sallie appearance-wise, and so, for the most part, she decided to give up trying. "I was thinking, since we have all this technology nowadays, let's make use of it, and see what we can find out from "Googling" all of the suspects. What do you think?"

"I think that's a great idea!" Sallie enthusiastically replied.

They both sat down at Arianna's dining room table and hovered over her laptop. Upon Sallie's request, the girls Googled Stanley Carter first. Unfortunately, the only thing they could find was a photo in a local newspaper of Stanley staring blankly into the camera, a befuddled expression on his face, as if he wasn't exactly sure where he was. Stanley had also apparently forgotten his teeth; therefore, looking like he could suck down an entire can of liquid Metamucil with his gums. Under the photo the caption read, "Stanley Carter - awarded, the '2009 Most Alert Octogenarian Prize' at the Meadowville Senior Center."

Sallie exclaimed, "Oh there's my Stanley! Doesn't he look cute?!"

"Yeah, that's not exactly the word I'd use but..." Arianna quickly plugged Paula La Paglia's name into Google. There was evidently no information regarding Paula La Paglia at all that they could find on the Web. "Dangit!" cried Arianna. "Let's see, who should we Google next? We don't have to Google my mother," she told Sallie. "I know she doesn't have any skeletons in her closet, she's the most boring and predictable person I can think of," Arianna explained.

Sallie nodded. "Okay, how about Camille Ciccone then?" she suggested. Arianna quickly typed her name into the search engine. They found a small somber looking picture of Camille wearing a conservative beige business suit, evidently taken when she worked at "Mayfair Manufacturing" as an executive secretary. They also discovered her resume on "LinkedIn".

"It looks like she only worked there for a year. Before that, she worked at a company in Cedarville, a northern suburb, for eighteen months as a secretary. I wonder why she was at those two places for such a short period of time? Let's call them on speakerphone and ask. I highly doubt we'll get an answer, but it's worth a try," Arianna said to Sallie.

When they called the office in Cedarville, the receptionist directed them to the director of human resources, a woman who said rather crankily, "I'm sorry, but it's our policy not to divulge that type of information," and hung up on them. When they called Mayfair Manufacturing, a woman answered and said that the human resources director was on vacation right now, but asked if they wanted to leave a message.

"No, but perhaps you could help us," Arianna said, in her most professional sounding manner. "We are evaluating Camille Ciccone as a possible job candidate for a secretarial position we have at our company. We see that she worked at your firm for a year, and just wanted to make certain that we would be making a wise choice, if we decided to hire her."

"Oh? What company are you from?" the inquisitive receptionist asked.

"Umm, Archer Tools and Manufacturing," she quickly replied.

"Oh, OK, what did you want to know?" she asked.

"Why was she only at your firm for two years? Did she quit?"

"Hmmm," she paused for a couple of seconds, "let's just say the executive she worked for had a problem with her."

"What kind of problem?" Arianna raised an eyebrow at Sallie.

A short silence followed. "There were personal issues that could not be reconciled and she did not leave the company by her own volition."

"I see, thank you very much for your help," she said, and hung up the phone.

"Wow!" Arianna said. "That's something, isn't it? I'm writing THAT little factoid down in my notebook."

Sallie stared at her confused. "I don't get it."

"Basically, what she was telling us was that Camille couldn't get along with her boss and was fired."

"Ohhh, well, why didn't she just say that?" Sallie said exasperatedly.

"I'll ask Mike to snoop around and find out exactly what happened there," Arianna confidently told her.

"How is Mike able to get so much information?" she asked.

"Mike knows EVERYBODY, has lots of friends and is owed a lot of favors," Arianna explained proudly. "He is a very valuable resource," she added. The thought then popped into her head that Mike's many friends were not limited to the male persuasion, and so Arianna was quiet for a little while after that.

The two women decided to move on to Rachel Gordon. While researching her, they discovered that Rachel had won third place in the "Best Apple Pie in Chicagoland" contest last year. "Damn, if I had known this, I would have taken her up on her offer to serve us refreshments yesterday," Arianna told Sallie, clearly upset with herself.

After taking a quick snack break, consisting of Pringles and Dr. Pepper, the girls realized that Arlene La Paglia had too many entries on the Internet to sift through all of them. There were many articles referencing her beautiful home, which had been featured on the annual "Great Estates" tour, which Somerset Hills arranged every year for the nosy, envious people who wanted to see how the other half lived. There were also tons of articles about and pictures of Arlene displayed on plenty of "Famous Models of the 1970's" websites. In all of her old modeling pics, Arlene appeared stunningly gorgeous. Just looking at them made Arianna feel even more insecure about her looks than usual. Arlene's hair was extremely long back then, golden with auburn highlights, and parted in the middle. In one picture, she was wearing an emerald-green chiffon dress which magnificently complemented her sapphire blue eyes and lightly freckled nose, neck and shoulders.

"Wow," said Sallie, "was she hot!"

"Yep, breathtaking," Arianna said, sighing. She then added, "And she STILL looks good for her age." (Arianna was young enough that it still surprised her, when anyone over fifty looked good.)

The most interesting thing they could find on any of the suspects, was an Esther Sullivan "YouTube" video they discovered, that garnered about 500,000 hits, of her lunging at her ex-husband in an open court scene. "You sonofabitch!" she screamed, her arms outstretched, as her lawyer and a guard tried to restrain her. They hauled her away kicking and screaming, and she was charged with contempt of court. She was forced to spend 48 hours in jail for her behavior.

"Man," said Sallie, "remind me never to make her mad!"

"Damn straight," Arianna replied, nodding her head.

Sallie said definitively, "She's almost certainly the killer."

"Oh?" Arianna looked at her expectantly.

"Look at all that pent-up rage," she explained.

"Yeah, but what would her motive be against Phil, specifically? It would have to be something pretty powerful to make her resort to murder. Especially, when you consider the fact that she never tried to kill her ex-husband, who she obviously despised."

"Who knows? Maybe she did try and kill her ex-husband but was unsuccessful. I don't know, but someone who behaves that way in public, definitely has a screw loose," Sallie said.

Arianna was nodding in agreement, when her phone started buzzing.

Feeling a little uneasy, she picked up. "Hi Mike."

"How's the investigation going Riann?"

"Great," Arianna said half-heartedly, looking at Sallie. "Sallie and I make a good team."

"I find that hard to believe," he told her.

Arianna ignored his comment. "Anyway, Sallie and I were Googling the suspects, and we discovered Camille got fired from her last job because she had some type of conflict with her boss. Who knows? Maybe she has an explosive temper, and she and Phil didn't see eye to eye on the secretarial job she did for him, he criticized her work, and she went bonkers and killed him?"

"That's kind of stretching it, don't you think? People criticize or offend one another countless times a day. If she was that nuts, she'd have killed hundreds, if not thousands, by now."

"Yeah, I guess you're right," Arianna said sighing, "but can you please look into this anyway?"

"Sure, anything else?" he asked.

"We also found a YouTube video of Esther in divorce court trying to physically assault her ex-husband. It was pretty intense. She actually had to serve a couple of days in the slammer for contempt."

"Well, I think we can safely assume Esther has a bit of a temper, that's for sure," he replied. "I wish I could do more to help you, but I am absolutely swamped here at work, Riann."

"That's okay, I understand." She took her phone into the other room, taking advantage of the fact that Sallie was occupied with Arianna's laptop. "Sooo, anything going on with you personally right now?" she asked him.

"What do you mean, personally?"

"I mean, like not work-related," she answered slightly frustrated.

"Nope, not really," he replied.

Her shoulders slumped. In a fake cheerful voice she said, "Well, I better go now, Sallie and I have lots of work to do." They said their goodbyes and she closed the phone.

"Well, it looks like we might have to follow the suspects, if we're going to catch any break in this case," she told Sallie, while walking back into the living room. "Maybe, we'll discover something new."

"But why? Didn't you interview them all already?" asked Sallie.

"Yes, but you can't trust anything people say, they could be hiding something. Remember what Dr. House says, 'everybody lies!'" Sallie had to admit she was right and soon departed, but agreed to return to Arianna's house that evening.

At 5:30 pm, Arianna answered the door wearing an auburn wig, horn-rimmed glasses, blue polyester pants and a matching short sleeved sweater top. Arianna had told Sallie to disguise herself and to be as inconspicuous as possible. However, to Arianna's dismay, she looked exactly the same as usual, incredibly sexy, in a tight white, extremely low-cut blouse, skin-tight white miniskirt, as short as you can get, and gold spiked four-inch heels.

"Why are you dressed like a lady of the evening?" Arianna immediately asked her.

"A what?" Sallie asked, confused.

"A whore," replied an annoyed Arianna. "What part of inconspicuous did you not understand?"

"I understood!" she indignantly replied.

"Then WHY are you so conspicuous?" she asked.

"You told me to come in disguise, and so I wore my hair up. I never wear my hair up," she explained.

"Aargh," Arianna cried, throwing up her hands, "we're going to have to disguise you better than that. I have a blond wig somewhere in here that I wore for Halloween one year." Arianna rummaged around her closet for a minute and got lucky. She handed a blond Dolly Parton-like wig to her. "Here put this on."

They both stood in front of Arianna's full-length mirror that hung from the back side of her bedroom door. "Oh my God, we look like Patsy and Eddy from Absolutely Fabulous!" Arianna exclaimed.

Absolutely Fabulous was a 1990's British comedy, starring Jennifer Saunders and Joanna Lumley as a pair of flighty, lazy, superficial, boozy, upper-middle class best friends. Comedy Central began running episodes of the pair's wacky mishaps and adventures several years ago. "Ab Fab", the abbreviation the show's fans use, was one of Arianna's favorite TV shows.

"Who's that?" asked Sallie.

"Oh Sallie, you have not lived until you've seen this TV show, it is HILARIOUS. I own all the episodes on DVD. Why don't you come over tomorrow night and bring Allen too, I'm sure he'll like it." Allen was Sallie's gay BFF.

"OK, that would be awesome!" Sallie enthusiastically exclaimed.

As they hopped into Arianna's car, Sallie asked, "Oh, by the way, how did the conversation with your mother go?"

"Eh, OK I guess. Didn't really learn anything except that Stanley went to the bathroom a lot that night which, by the way, Rachel had also mentioned."

Sallie nodded. "Yes, I'm sure he did. You would not believe how many times he has to go to the bathroom at night. It's a little frustrating because he wakes me up and…"

Arianna interrupted, "So, who do you think we should follow first?"

"How about your mother?" suggested Sallie.

"My mother?" Arianna asked.

"Well, she's supposedly a suspect too, you said, and you've already interviewed her and didn't learn anything useful, so why not?"

Arianna couldn't argue with that logic, so they drove to a spot a half a block away from Sandra Archer's house. Arianna was driving her own car, because Sallie's car, like Sallie, was extremely conspicuous. It was hot pink, the exact color of Pepto Bismol, and everyone around Meadowville knew that Sallie Rigelli owned it. Arianna had brought an expensive pair of binoculars that she was looking through at the moment, which was trained on her mother's front door. A half an hour later, when Sandra Archer left her house and got into her car, Arianna handed off the binoculars to Sallie and began to follow her in hot pursuit.

While speeding through the streets of Meadowville, Arianna asked, "Now, what exactly do we think my mother is going to do, walk into a 'Murderers Anonymous' meeting?" Sallie shrugged her shoulders.

They followed Sandra until she stopped in front of a local pharmacy, got out of her car, and walked inside. Arianna parked in the lot next door and the two women followed a safe distance behind. Sallie whispered excitedly, "Oh my gosh, what if she's purchasing some sort of dangerous drug? We have to find out!" Arianna looked at her skeptically. The two decided to walk in separately and station themselves near the prescription pick-up window.

"Here you go," said the pharmacist to Mrs. Archer, "do you have any questions about the medication?"

"Yes, young man I do, I've heard that this painkiller for my back may cause headaches, is that true? I don't need any more headaches. I have enough as it is, with my eldest daughter."

Arianna moaned in protest, but then remembering she didn't want to draw attention to herself, quickly put her hand over her mouth. She walked quietly over to Sallie and whispered, "I think we've heard enough. She's obviously just picking up a painkiller for her back. Let's go."

Just as Sallie was about to respond, they heard a familiar voice behind them. "Arianna, what are you doing in that hideous wig? And you are Sallie Rigelli, I presume?"

Arianna and Sallie turned around and looked at her with guilty expressions on their faces. "How did you know we were here?" Arianna asked her sheepishly.

"Oh, I saw your car tailing me, dear. For someone who reads so many mysteries, you should really learn how to tail a suspect better. Perhaps Michael could give you lessons in his free time?" she suggested.

Arianna stood there embarrassed and fuming, while Sallie smiled and said, "Hi Mrs. Archer, nice to meet you."

"Hello Ms. Rigelli, I don't particularly care for your wig either, but that is a very fine quality blouse, where did you buy it?"

"Thank you, it's Donna Karan. I work down on Michigan Avenue and I get great discounts," Sallie replied with enthusiasm.

"Really? How wonderful. I've told Arianna a thousand times she should look into working at a high-end store in the city, but she never listens." The two of them began having an in-depth conversation regarding clothes, while Arianna drifted about, sighing loudly and repeatedly and growing more and more impatient.

"OK, I think we're done here Sallie, let's go. See you Mom," she said, practically dragging Sallie out the door.

"Sorry, have to go, bye!" Sallie managed to squeak out, waving back at Sandra.

"Goodbye you two, take care. Remember, next time try and manage to do a much better job if you're planning on spying on anyone else," she reprimanded them.

As the pair returned to the car, Sallie said, "Riann, I don't think we should do any more of this spying. We don't seem to be any good at it," she said, as way of an explanation, while Arianna silently fuming, did not answer. They drove back to Arianna's house in silence. When they arrived back at Arianna's, Sallie said, while searching for her car keys, "Have a great night, see you tomorrow. I can't wait to tell Allen about 'Ab Fab' when I get home!"

Arianna, still feeling embarrassed by her mother, feigned enthusiasm, "Me either, good night!" and entered her house, slamming the door behind her.

The following evening, Arianna was nervous about having to entertain Sallie and Allen. The truth is, she didn't have any close friends really, except for Mike. Arianna was not a people person, and there were very few she tolerated enough to keep company with. She usually preferred TV shows and books to humans, so the prospect of entertaining them both in her home was proving a little stressful for her. She wasn't sure what she should wear to an 'Ab Fab' marathon either, and so was dressed more formally than was probably necessary, in a long, lavender, short-sleeved sweater dress, which featured a giant cowl around her neck.

At 7:00 pm on the dot, Sallie and Allen arrived, bringing two bottles of *Moscato d'Asti* with them, a wine all three coincidentally happened to love. It was also proven later to go surprisingly well with the popcorn Arianna had made and served up in small, dark blue, Rachael Ray dinnerware bowls. "Hello, come in," she welcomed the pair into her home. She turned to Allen and extended her hand, "Hi,

I'm Arianna, it's so nice to finally meet you. I'm so glad you could both make it."

Allen, who was wearing a bright yellow, long-sleeved shirt and tight, white shorts, which complemented his strawberry blond hair and golden tan, shook her hand and said, "I'm Allen, and it's a pleasure to meet you sweetie, I could not wait until tonight! I told Sallie, 'What? An 'Ab Fab' marathon? I wouldn't miss it for the world!'"

Three episodes and plenty of wine, chatting, and laughter later, the doorbell rang. Arianna, a tad perplexed, as she was not expecting more company, looked through the peephole and saw that it was Mike. She answered the door, a little flushed, "Hey, what's up?"

"Nothing much. Just finished my shift and wanted to see how everything was going. Why are you so dressed up?" He peered inside curiously. "You have company?"

"Oh yeah, Sallie Rigelli and her friend Allen." Arianna walked Mike into the living room and introduced him. "Allen, this is my friend Mike."

"Well, well, well, I DO love a man in uniform. Too bad you're on the wrong side," he twittered and went back to watching 'Ab Fab'. Sallie waved flirtatiously at him.

"Hello folks. I'll let you get back to, well, whatever it is that you're watching," Mike said, looking as if he couldn't wait to get out of there.

"Absolutely Fabulous," Arianna informed him, as she walked him to the door.

"I can't believe you're actually having people over, what's got into you?" Mike whispered to her, as soon as they were both back in her front doorway.

"Hey, sometimes you just have to mix things up a little," she replied mysteriously.

"Alright Miss Adventurous, how did the interview with your mother go?"

Arianna filled him in and then said, "We even spied on her to see if any of her movements were suspicious.

"What? Listen Riann, I'm not really worried about you tailing Sandra, but it is NOT a good idea to start spying on the other suspects. It could be very dangerous, and at the very least, you could get the police department in trouble for invasion of privacy. Promise me you won't tail anyone else," he told her.

"Alright," she agreed, a little too quickly, Mike noticed, and immediately grew suspicious.

"So, what did happen when you and Sallie followed Sandra?" he inquired.

"Well, she made us," Arianna admitted, obviously embarrassed.

"Really? Tell me what happened."

She recounted the whole story and Mike laughed so hard, he doubled over and developed a stitch in his side. "I fail to see what's so humorous," she said very stiffly.

"Oh, Riann," he cried, and began laughing again.

"Well, I'm sorry, I have to go. I have an 'Ab Fab' marathon I've got to get back to."

"OK," he said, trying desperately to stop laughing. "I'll see you later."

"Bye, have a good night," she called after him as he walked down her front steps. *That's great, now I'll be the laughingstock of the Meadowville Police Department.*

When she came back inside, both Sallie and Allen were smiling at her. "So, I hear that hunka hunka burning love is your man. Lucky girl!" said Allen.

"Ah, well…, never mind," she replied, blushing furiously. "Uh, let's get back to the show."

Suddenly, the song, "Bad Girls" by Donna Summer, blasted throughout the room. Arianna was very confused, but soon realized it was Sallie's phone. Sallie struggled to find it in her handbag, then picked up. "Oh hi! Yes? Oh, I'm sorry I can't, I'm actually at Riann's right now. Umm, yes, her house does look clean," Sallie replied, her eyes scanning the room. Arianna stared at her suspiciously. "How about tomorrow during the day sometime? I have off from work. Good, I'll call you tomorrow morning then. *Ciao*!" She ended the call and looked up to see Arianna staring at her expectantly.

"So, who was that?" she asked.

"Sandy, I mean, your mom," Sallie replied.

"You, you call her Sandy, and she's okay with that?" she asked, astounded.

"Of course, she doesn't mind at all," Sallie answered. "I felt badly for following her, so I called her last night to apologize, and we ended up talking like, for hours. Oh by the way, you didn't tell me your dad was so much older than your mom. It turns out Sandy and I have lots in common. I don't know why you're always complaining about her, she is so cool."

"Cool?" Arianna repeated weakly, thinking she must have entered the Twilight Zone or Superman's "Bizarro" world. Whatever the case may be, she decided another glass of *Moscato d' Asti* was in order, post-haste.

Chapter Fourteen - The Wake

The next morning, trying to fend off the headache she had developed due to her excessive *Moscato* intake the night before, Arianna gulped down three ibuprofen tablets with a glass of orange juice. She then grabbed the laptop off her kitchen counter and took it to bed with her. As soon as it was powered up, she logged on to her Facebook page. Just out of curiosity, Arianna occasionally looked at her ex-coworkers' pages to see what was going on with them. After glancing over a few, it appeared as if more of them got laid off, and that the company they had all worked so diligently for, was about to fold. She didn't wish anyone hard luck, but, as they say, "misery does love company."

She also noticed she had one message from Sallie, informing her that Phil's wake was set for tomorrow, and one new "Friend Request" from a Sandra Rose. Hmm, that's my mother's name, she thought, small world. Arianna clicked on Sandra Rose's profile, and exclaimed, "Oh my God!" She was looking at her mother's freshly created Facebook page. Her profile pic featured a much younger Sandra Archer, with a bouffant hairdo and a navy blue blouse, which featured a starched white, Peter Pan collar. The picture appeared very formal and her mother had a grim expression on her face (which, according to her oldest daughter, was her only facial expression). Arianna was quite familiar with the photo, for it was her mother's high school graduation picture taken back in 1966.

Arianna personally made it a point to never use a photo of herself as her profile picture, mainly because she was inarguably unphotogenic. She couldn't tell you how many instances there have been, where upon meeting her for the first time, someone told her in a surprised voice, "Oh, you're actually quite decent-looking in person." Instead, she always used a photo of a television show character as her profile pic. Currently, it was Jaclyn Smith's, "Kelly Garrett" from Charlie's Angels, circa 1977. Charlie's Angels was yet another favorite TV show Arianna first became exposed to years after it began running in syndication. Arianna's favorite angel was Kelly, because Sabrina was too mannish and Jill seemed too dumb, although she did concede that

Farrah Fawcett's, "Jill Munroe" was the most attractive. Arianna would have died for that hair.

In fact, one time when she had a bad case of the flu as a pre-teen and thought she was dying, she instructed her parents to make sure that she had "Farrah" hair at her wake. Like with most of Arianna's instructions, her parents just replied, "Yes, dear," and to her consternation, never even wrote them down or gave them any consideration whatsoever. Because of this, over the years, she made sure to tell Mike exactly how her hair should look, what clothes she should be wearing and what songs should be playing at her wake/memorial service, if she should die before him. (She said either "My Heart Will Go On" (Theme from Titanic) by Celine Dion or "The Way We Were" by Barbra Streisand would be appropriate, as long as a slideshow of pre-approved pictures of her were flashing up on a giant screen above her casket. He had sarcastically asked her if she wanted him to hire professional mourners as well. Unfortunately for Mike, the sarcasm was lost on Arianna and she replied, "Oh, do you know a place where you can hire those people? Is it expensive?"

She scrolled down to see what "Sandra Rose" had listed as her Favorite Activities. "Billiards, Bunco, and Mahjong," she read. "Mahjong? What the hell is Mahjong?" she said aloud. Oh my God, this is so embarrassing, she thought. She clasped her hand over her mouth and scanned down to what her mother had listed as her Favorite Books: Emily Post's Etiquette and Miss Manners Guide to Excruciatingly Correct Behavior. *How utterly horrible.* Under movies Sandra had listed one, "The Sound of Music." *Ugh, how boring.* It was only going from bad to worse for Arianna. Finally, she couldn't take anymore, so she logged off. She was left shocked, dazed, and confused. Sandra thought Facebook was crass. She had remarked many times in the past that it was repulsive how so many people put themselves out there and hung out their dirty laundry for all to see. *What the hell is happening? My world is falling apart!* She closed her laptop and tried to regain her composure.

Once somewhat composed, she called Mike and told him about the budding relationship between her mom and Sallie and the monstrosity on Facebook that she had just discovered.

149

"Well, I have to say, I can't think of an odder couple than Sandra and Sallie. Oh wait, yes I can, Stanley and Sallie." He chuckled at his own joke.

Arianna wasn't in a joking mood. "I blame Sallie for this Facebook nightmare, she has turned out to be a very destructive influence on my mom."

Unfortunately, Mike wasn't as supportive and understanding about this as she had thought he would be. "Calm down Riann, you should be happy for your mother. Good for her, finally putting herself out there."

"I don't want her out there, it's bad enough she's in here! The rest of the world shouldn't have to be subjected to her."

"OK, I'm hanging up now," said Mike.

"Hey, I'm still talk…," she heard the sound of a click. "Argh!" she said aloud and immediately called her mother.

"Arianna you haven't accepted my Friend Request yet," she complained, as soon as she picked up the phone.

Shoot, Arianna thought. *Well, maybe I can accept her Friend Request, but under Relatives, I'll list her as a great aunt. That way people would understand that I wouldn't of my own volition, purposely choose her as a friend, but that I'm only doing it because she's a family member. A great aunt would also be far away enough genetically, that people wouldn't automatically jump to the conclusion, that I'VE also got the crazy gene.*

"Why Mom, why would you set up a Facebook account?" she whined.

"Sallie Rigelli told me this is the best method of attracting a gentleman caller."

I knew it, she thought, I knew Sallie had to be behind this. *Gentleman caller, what kind of archaic lingo is that? Does she think she's in a Tennessee Williams play? Maybe she should start dating Stanley.* "Why the interest in gentlemen callers all of a sudden? And by the way, if you think that photo's going to attract some guy, you're nuts," Arianna told her mother.

"Let me be the judge of that, and why would I listen to you anyway? Looking at your track record with men, I'd hardly take your opinion as gospel."

"Good point," Arianna conceded. "Listen, I just found out Phil La Paglia's wake is set for tomorrow night."

"So?"

Arianna sighed. "Well, the reason I called is, I wanted to see if you were going or not."

"Why would I go to Phil's wake, I hardly knew the man?" she asked her.

"Well, it's been lovely talking to you as usual, Mother," she said sarcastically, and closed the phone. Knowing she would never hear the end of it if she didn't, she reluctantly accepted her mom's Friend Request.

Arianna really wanted to go to the wake, not only to pay her respects, but she thought it might be beneficial for their investigation. However, she didn't want to go alone and she didn't want to ask Mike. She was too afraid he'd tell her he had other plans, and then she'd be worrying that his other plans meant he was spending time with Barbara. She also didn't want to ask Sallie, because she knew she'd be going with Stanley, and she didn't think she could handle his snail-like pace for too long. She could call Emily, but she didn't think attending a wake for a man she never even met, would be much of a draw for her. Looks like she was flying solo for this one, she thought.

The next morning, because nothing fit her anymore, Arianna decided to bite the bullet and buy a new black dress for Phil's wake. She decided to shop at where Sallie worked, "La Boutique Exclusif", a high-end department store on Michigan Avenue in downtown Chicago.

However, when Arianna got there, she became frustrated really fast, because she had forgotten that all these high-end boutiques in the city catered specifically to thin, petite, rich women, who have enough money for things like trainers and cooks. They could also afford to consistently eat a healthy diet and not cheap convenience junk food, like the rest of the peons, including Arianna, did. The store didn't have one dress that would fit a 5'10" woman with actual hips and breasts.

She whined to Sallie, "Nothing here fits me," as she walked over to her with a bunch of rejected dresses draped over her left arm. Arianna noticed Sallie was dressed slightly less provocatively at work, in a dark blue, low-cut (but not obscene), knee-length, form-fitting dress and matching shoes.

"Oh," Sallie, who was busy dressing mannequins in clothes that only runway models would have the courage to wear, said, "you need to look through our 'BBW' rack, which we keep in the back of the store. Don't worry, I'm sure we'll find something that fits you there."

"BBW? What's that stand for?" she asked.

"Big Boned Woman rack," she replied, slightly uncomfortable. Arianna, predictably, was irked but when she found the perfect dress there right away, her countenance brightened considerably. When she came out of the dressing room and twirled around a couple of times in front of her, Sallie cried, "Oh, you look so beautiful!" Arianna was wearing a black dress with a gold belt and gold buttons lined down the front. She was excited because she knew she had some black heels with gold straps at home which would go perfect with it. The dress had already been marked down twice, plus Sallie gave her a 20% discount, so Arianna got it for a steal. The dress accentuated Arianna's ample bosom, and created the illusion of her waist being smaller. When she had it on, she felt like a femme fatale, so needless to say, she was very pleased with her purchase. After buying the dress, she noticed that Sallie was pretty busy, so she left the store soon afterwards.

That evening, Arianna drove to Phil's wake, held at Somerset Hills Funeral Parlor, from 4:00 pm to 9:00 pm. On the way there, she got held up by a group of cyclists. Among Arianna's biggest pet peeves, were people who rode bicycles, not kids or old people, or normal everyday folk who ride down sidewalks or residential streets, but specifically, Lance Armstrong wannabes who were anorexically thin, and wore professional looking bike helmets and black spandex shorts. These dumbasses, as Arianna liked to refer to them, travelled in packs like wolves, and tried to outrun traffic on busy streets during rush hour. When Arianna was still employed by the book distribution firm where she spent twelve years, she would have to take a 45 mph four lane street, with two lanes running in each direction to work. Every day, like clockwork, a whole pack of these men would ride as fast as they could in the right lane, pedaling as if they were competing in the *Tour de France*. Therefore, if a car was already in the right lane behind them, they were forced to either swerve into the left lane quickly, which most of the time during rush hour is pretty difficult, or virtually come to a complete stop, waiting for someone to let them cut in front of them in the left lane. Otherwise, they would have to crawl behind the pack, tailing them at 2 mph, hoping that the cyclists would eventually turn down a side street.

Now, Chicagoland suburbs are filled with forest preserve paths and bike trails that these men could use, if they cared about anyone other than themselves, according to Arianna, but instead they preferred to add at least five minutes to everyone else's commutes to and from work. She believed there was a special place in Hell for these men. Arianna would rant that they did this seven days a week, morning and evening, spring, summer, and fall, no matter what the weather was like, always in the same stupid tight little Spandex outfits. Even though there was nobody else in the car and the men couldn't hear her, she'd call them every swear word you could think of, plus some truly innovative ones that she'd make up on the spot. She'd wonder, don't these asswipes work? How can they afford to bike all day? These men are too young to be retired, is there a whole breed of independently wealthy cyclists out there? Arianna literally could, and did, bitch about them for hours to anyone who'd listen. She had tried many times to get Mike to arrest them, but to her dismay, he'd say, "How many times do I have to tell you, they aren't doing anything illegal Riann!" He wouldn't understand anyway, she'd tell herself. He's a cop, when people see him coming, they automatically try to avoid him and jump out of his way. Now these idiots were riding around at 7:30 at night and she was livid. *Goddamn assholes!* As she changed lanes and then came back to cut them off, Arianna yelled out her window, "Get a life!"

She arrived at the funeral parlor around 7:55 pm filled with dread. She hated wakes, especially those that were open casket. It seemed to her that after the mortician got through with them, everyone ended up looking like a wax mannequin. She noticed Mike was already there paying his respects, holding his police cap in his hands and looking really cute. He saw Arianna and did a double-take. Not only did the new dress make her figure look fantastic, but she had curled her naturally straight hair so that it was long and bouncy, very Farrah-like. She nodded at him politely; however, she was secretly thrilled, for it was obvious to her from the expression on his face and the way he was staring, that he wanted to jump her bones. She walked slowly towards the body, which was laid out in an expensive casket, made of a beautiful rich mahogany wood and draped with yellow roses, white lilies and purple lilacs. Then she became sidetracked, because Esther Sullivan had just stormed through the door of the funeral parlor, walking at a very rapid pace. She was wearing brown designer sunglasses and an expensive V-necked, long-sleeved, red blouse with black slacks. Esther didn't go near the coffin at all, she noticed, she just circled the room once like a vulture and then tried to leave. To her dismay, Arianna ran up to her before that could happen.

"Hi Esther," she stopped her, "nice to see you again. Boy, I sure hate wakes, don't you?"

Looking everywhere but at Arianna, she mumbled, "I suppose so," and she started once again heading towards the door.

"Leaving so soon?"

"Yes," she said flatly.

"May I ask why?" inquired Arianna.

"I've got places to go, excuse me," she said brusquely, and walked quickly past her out of the building.

Arianna sighed, then turned back around. I'm sure Arlene and Paula are somewhere around here, she thought. *Ah, there's Arlene.* She watched as Arlene La Paglia, dressed in a pretty yellow pantsuit with a white scarf around her neck and yellow slingbacks on her feet, walked up to Phil's body, looked around surreptitiously, and slipped a piece of paper into the casket.

Arianna snuck quietly up behind her, "Hello Arlene, how are things going? Are you holding up alright?"

"Yes, I'm doing okay in spite of the circumstances, I guess," she replied.

"I couldn't help but notice you placed a piece of paper in the casket," Arianna casually remarked.

Arlene appeared startled and not too pleased. "What? Oh, it's a letter Phil wrote to me many years ago, during some happier times. I felt like it belonged with him," she explained and turning her back on her, walked away.

Mike, who had overheard the exchange, walked up to Arianna. "Have you no shame?" he said, frowning at her.

"What are you talking about?" she asked, confused.

"This is a wake, Riann. The sleuthing can wait until later."

"Hmmph," she replied and walked away. *Obviously, Mike isn't as much of a professional as I thought. Nothing should get in the way of an official police investigation, not even a wake.* She didn't see anyone else she knew except for Camille Ciccone, who was decked out all in black, wearing a black silk shirt, black polyester pants and black flats. She had been kneeling at Phil's casket for at least five minutes. What a casket hogger, Arianna thought. She had wanted to pay her respects and say a quick prayer at Phil's casket before she left the wake, but Camille wouldn't get up. She was trying to be patient, but as anyone who knew Arianna was well aware, patience was not one of her strong suits, or actually any of her suits, for that matter. Ten minutes later, she was just about to tap Camille on the shoulder, or shove her off the kneeler, Arianna hadn't made a final decision yet, when she finally got up. Arianna gave her a dirty look, but Camille didn't seem to notice. She walked up and kneeled down next to the casket. As she expected, Phil La Paglia resembled a wax mannequin, albeit a good-looking one. He was dressed in an expensive black suit with a white carnation pinned to his lapel. After a minute or so, she got up, and at the urging of her pea-sized bladder, figured she'd better use the restroom, just in case.

As she entered the first stall, she noticed Camille at one of the three sinks washing her hands vigorously, as if she were about to perform surgery. When Arianna finished her business, Camille was still at the sink scrubbing her hands. After Arianna washed her own hands and had dried them under the hand dryer attached to the wall, Camille was still at it. She shook her head as she exited the restroom, leaving Camille maniacally scrubbing at the sink. *What an obsessive compulsive nutcase.*

Arianna noticed there was quite a number of people there, which was a little surprising, since Phil didn't seem to have many close friends. She figured many of them were probably friends or family of Arlene's, since Arlene was starting to draw quite a crowd of sad-looking people, all offering their condolences. Arianna realized she hadn't seen Paula, Sarah, or Rachel at all, and decided to check out the signature book to see if they had perhaps, signed in earlier. *Hmm, there's Paula La Paglia's name, she was here quite early, but there's no record of the other two ladies paying their respects.* Well, she thought, I'd better not assume anything, maybe they just forgot to sign it. *I don't want to bother Arlene again, I'll see if Mike's still around.*

Arianna spotted him right away in the middle of a discussion with some other cop, whom she had never seen before. They looked like they were discussing something extremely serious. She sauntered up to them, and in her deep, throaty, sexy voice said, "Excuse me, when you gentlemen are finished, may I have a word with you Mike?"

Mike looked at her curiously. "Hey Tom, I'll talk to you later OK?"

Tom, a tall, middle-aged man with brown eyes and dark brown hair sprinkled with flecks of gray, looked Arianna up and down appreciatively. "No problem at all," he replied.

"You can finish your conversation you know, I can wait," she magnanimously offered.

"No, that's alright I have some calls to make anyway. See ya Mike," he said, as he walked away.

"See you later!" Arianna smiled and waved goodbye to him.

"OK, Marilyn Monroe, what do you want?" Mike warily asked her.

"Who was that?" Arianna asked.

"Oh, uh Tom Manfrey, an old friend of mine who works for the Somerset Hills Police Department. He lives only a few houses down from Phil and had decided to pay his respects," he said, averting his eyes.

"Oh? How come I never heard you mention him before?" she asked curiously.

"I have, you've probably just forgotten," appearing shifty, he replied.

She stared at him. "Why are you acting so weird?"

"Riann, did you come over here for a reason or what?" he answered, his tone turning testy.

Why do I get the feeling he's lying? I really think this investigation is starting to mess with my head. Why on earth would Mike lie about knowing some cop? "Oh, well anyway," she resumed her sexy voice, "I was wondering if you could tell me if Sarah Brewster or Rachel Gordon showed up here tonight?"

"Ohhh, so you need my help huh? Well, lucky for you, you're looking so sexy, that I have no choice, I am literally powerless to do anything, but help you out baby," he told her, turning on the charm. Arianna turned red, but then began wondering if he had been turning on the same charm for his ex-wife lately. "I've been here for the last two hours and neither woman was here during that time. I'll go and check with Sgt. Tennyson though. He's been stationed outside since the wake began."

Mike turned to leave, but she stopped him with a question. "I don't understand, why have you been here so long and why is Sgt. Tennyson here?"

He explained, "When a murder has taken place, most often the perp comes to the wake or funeral to inspect his handiwork, so it's standard operating procedure for the cops to attend the wake, and more often than not, take the names of the people who come to the visitation."

"That's right, I should have remembered that from all the Criminal Minds episodes I've watched, I must be slipping. I did notice John standing outside, but I didn't know that's what he was doing," she told him. "Why didn't he ask me for my name though?"

"Because he knows who you are silly, it's either that or he was simply transfixed by how sexy you look in that dress," he said, winking at her flirtatiously. She blushed again. "Wait here, I'll be right back," Mike told her.

A couple of minutes later he returned. "Nope, neither woman has come to the wake tonight."

"Thanks Mike, I appreciate it," Arianna said, starting to walk away, when she whipped back around suddenly. "Oh shit!" she exclaimed, clapping her hand to her forehead. "I totally forgot about Stanley Carter. Do you know if he was here?"

"Oh yes, actually he and Sallie Rigelli left right before you got here," he said, smirking a little.

"Oh? Did I miss anything," she asked curiously.

"I would say so, quite a lot, actually," he replied. Knowing not only how impatient she was, but how much she loved gossip, Mike was taking pleasure in dragging every bit of information out as much as possible.

"Oh no, what happened?" she asked, not completely sure if she really wanted to know.

Mike went over the sequence of events with her. "Well, the lovely couple caused quite a stir. Sallie shocked everyone by wearing, what appeared to be a black blouse and five inch gold heels."

"A black blouse, so what? Was she wearing a skirt with it or pants?" Arianna asked, confused.

"When I say she was wearing a black blouse, I mean that was ALL she was wearing. The blouse ended extremely high on her upper thigh."

"What?" she cried, clearly appalled. She put her hands on her hips. "Surely, she was wearing underwear?"

"I can't speak to that personally, since as you know, I am a perfect gentleman, but... I just happened to overhear a few of the ladies around here discussing it, purely by accident of course..."

Arianna said, "Oh of course. Now go on...," she prodded him, becoming impatient.

"And the ladies commented that it was quite apparent to them, that she might have, let's say, 'forgotten'," Mike used air quotes, "to put on a brassiere this evening."

"Oh Lord," Arianna replied, feeling a twinge of jealousy. Knowing that Mike got an eyeful of that, made her feel much less confident, despite her sexy dress, of her own physical appeal.

"Anyway," he continued, "Sallie began weeping uncontrollably as soon as she reached Phil's casket…"

"But she never even met Phil!" she said, raising her voice. Arianna never had any patience for people who cry hysterically at funerals. She always thought they should be happy that the deceased were able to depart this crazy-ass world, as she liked to put it.

Mike shrugged his shoulders. "Just telling you what happened."

"How was Stanley taking everything, did he start crying too? Well, if he did, HE at least, has an excuse for doing so," she said.

"What do you mean? I was under the impression that he only knew Phil from serving him a few drinks at the dances?"

"Well, he's his father, wouldn't you expect him to be upset if his son died?"

"What? What are you talking about?" Mike asked her, sounding excited, but bewildered at the same time.

"What do you mean, what am I talking about? Ohhh yeahh, I forgot to tell you," she said, turning red, "I found out Stanley was Phil's biological father." Arianna proceeded to fill him in on everything Sallie had told her.

"I can't believe you withheld valuable information like this," Mike replied, clearly annoyed.

"I didn't do it on purpose, and besides, it's not like you've never withheld information from me before," she defended herself.

"What does that mean? I've given you all the information I have on this case."

"Whatever. Listen, I honestly forgot, I've been busy,"

"Yeah, I know, watching Ab Fab marathons, pretty hard life you have," he replied, uncharacteristically nasty. Arianna just stared at him, feeling hurt and more than a little puzzled.

"Well, now I'm going to have to look into Stanley's finances. Even though Phil's death won't affect him financially, maybe he didn't know that." Mike paused for a second and then continued, "You know Riann, Ed still put me in charge of the investigation and…"

"OK, OK, sorry," she interrupted, "please go on with the story about Sallie and Stanley you were in the middle of telling me."

"Alright," a little less angry, he continued, "Stanley tried to console Sallie, and a few minutes later, she had stopped crying, parked herself on his lap, and shoved her tongue down his throat."

"Ick!" squealed Arianna.

"Ick is right," Mike agreed. "Everyone had pretty much the same reaction. Then Sallie began telling him quite loudly, what she wanted to do to him sexually when they got home."

"Oh my God, I can't believe you didn't tell me all this right away! Even Sallie isn't usually that brash, something must be the matter with her."

"Well, I think she just might have had a drink or two," he explained. "According to my sources, she was telling people that wakes and funerals always make her break down crying, and so she decided to have a few drinks before the wake first to calm her nerves."

"Oh, this is terrible." Arianna put her hands on her head and started pacing back and forth in front of him.

"Wait, you don't want to miss the best part," he said, grinning.

"There's more?" she asked painfully.

"Yep, unfortunately, every time she'd say something sexually suggestive to Stanley, he would respond by yelling, 'What? I can't hear you!' and she'd have to repeat herself, word for word, even louder. Finally, a couple of women went over to them and asked that they leave because they were making too much of a spectacle of themselves."

"Oh, I bet that didn't go over very well."

"No, actually they were both okay with it, as they appeared to be pretty, umm, how do I put this delicately, 'randy' and were more than ready to go home together."

Arianna put her hand on her stomach and her face was beginning to turn an interesting shade of pea green. "Uhh, I feel nauseous," she moaned.

"I'm guessing most of the people here felt the same way," he said.

"Alright, change of subject please," she told him. "I think it's pretty odd that neither Sarah, nor Rachel showed up tonight, and the wake is almost over. Especially Sarah, she seems like the type of person that always does the right thing, and attending the wake would be the proper thing to do. Sarah's actually the kind of woman who would probably even try and take charge of the whole thing."

"From what you've told me about her, I'd have to agree. So you are going to get to the bottom of that, I presume?" Mike asked her.

"Yep! I'll give you the scoop tomorrow."

Arianna said goodbye to Mike and left the funeral home. Oh what a mess, she thought. *So much for calling Sallie tomorrow and asking her if she observed anyone acting suspiciously tonight. I doubt she'll be in any condition to even remember tonight. This unequivocally sucks, and if her relationship with Stanley lasts any longer, I'm going to have to start taking Dramamine.*

Before she pulled away from the funeral parlor parking lot; however, Arianna decided she couldn't wait, but would call Sarah and Rachel immediately and see what excuse they give for not coming to

Phil's wake. She pulled out her cell phone and called Sarah Brewster first. After five rings, Sarah answered sounding groggy. "Hello?"

"Hi Sarah, this is Arianna Archer. I hope it's not too late to call." Arianna heard a big sigh on the other end of the line.

"I was sleeping, I hope this is really important," she said, sounding extremely pissed off.

"Welll, I, I," Arianna stammered, taken by surprise by Sarah's unusually angry tone, "I'm just leaving Phil La Paglia's wake and I heard that you hadn't made it out here tonight. I was wondering if you were doing alright."

"I'm fine," she said shortly. "I just came down at the last minute with the stomach flu, and I thought it was best not to risk going out. So I took it easy this evening and went to bed early, until of course, I was interrupted by this phone call."

"Oh, OK, well, I'll let you get back to your sleep then," she replied sheepishly.

"Arianna, I hope these questions you have for me do not become a regular occurrence. I'm beginning to feel this is bordering on harassment. Didn't your mother raise you better than this?" Not waiting for an answer, she slammed the phone down.

"Yikes!" Arianna said aloud, sticking her finger in her right ear to stop the ringing. What a Mrs. Crankypants, she thought. *Well, I hope it goes a little better with Rachel.* She quickly pushed in Rachel's phone number.

"Hello?" Rachel answered on the second ring. Well, Arianna thought with some relief, she certainly sounds awake enough.

"Hi Rachel, this is Arianna Archer." There was silence on the other end of the line. "I'm just leaving Phil's wake and I noticed you weren't here tonight." Again, silence. "I, I," she stuttered, feeling very uncomfortable, "was worried there might be something wrong."

Rachel quietly replied, "No, there isn't."

A little perplexed, Arianna said to her, "Oh, I'm just a little surprised, I thought you liked Phil."

There was a pause, and then Rachel said in a very snippy, un Rachel-like, tone of voice, "I don't go to wakes or funerals. If the whole town suddenly died, I still wouldn't attend the memorial service. Is there anything else?"

"No, thank…," she started to say, then realized Rachel had already hung up. *Well, I'm now two for two. I seem to be making enemies left and right here. Geez, I thought old people were supposed to have such good manners. Just another urban myth, I guess…*

Chapter Fifteen - Bowling

The next morning, Arianna was awakened by a phone call. She looked over at the alarm clock. It was 9:45 am. Hmmm, which one of my friends or family members has a death wish, she thought. She reached over and picked up her phone.

"Riann, it's Sallie."

"Sallie?" Arianna sat up alarmed, "did something bad happen?"

"No, everything is fine. I just wanted to ask you something before you had time to make any other plans."

"Oh?" she asked warily.

"I was talking to Stanley and telling him how much of a good time I had with you the other night, and he suggested we go on a double date with you and Mike tonight."

"Well, as I've mentioned before, Mike and I are not dating right now, so it would probably feel pretty awkward to go on a double date with you guys," she explained to her. "We're only working together on this investigation, that's all." Sallie pooh-poohed Arianna's concerns and continued making plans. Arianna was in the middle of trying to formulate another excuse in her head, when she heard the word "bowling". "Did you say bowling?" she asked Sallie.

"Yes! It turns out Stanley was a champion bowler when he was young, and he loves bowling."

"Oh, well in that case, sure why not, we'll bowl with you guys," she replied.

"Shouldn't you ask Mike first?" Sallie asked, concerned.

"Oh, I know Mike will absolutely say yes, he loves to bowl," Arianna assured her.

"Well, in that case, awesome! We'll meet you at Chestnut Peaks Bowling Alley at 7 pm."

"Umm Sallie, before I forget, there is something I want to talk to you about," she told her.

"Oh?" She sounded nervous.

"Yes, I heard you caused a little scene last night, and..."

Sallie interrupted her, "Oh Arianna I know, I'm so embarrassed. I just had a little too much to drink, and well, that's what happens when I have too much to drink. I get extremely emotional and horny and I..."

Arianna cut her off, "I know, I know, but I want us to look professional, so that Mike takes us seriously. I don't want him thinking that we're running around drinking and carousing all the time. Also, it would be helpful if maybe you could take it down a notch with the sexy clothing?"

"Arianna, my outfit was NOT that bad, I even wore panties and everything."

"Alright, alright, see you tonight then, and thanks for the invite." Arianna closed the phone and immediately called Mike.

"Stevenson," he answered on the first ring.

"Hi Mike, I just talked to Sallie and...," she proceeded to tell him about their plans.

"Absolutely not!" he firmly replied. Mike Stevenson took his bowling very seriously. He was a fantastic bowler and never bowled under a 200, as long as Arianna had known him, which was about sixteen years.

Arianna and Mike first crossed paths sixteen years ago when she was causing quite a ruckus at the Meadowville Library. According to the official police record, Arianna had been in line to check out a book and there was some young couple in front of her checking out around twenty-five VHS tapes. She became impatient and couldn't understand why someone would take out that many movies at one time. She also couldn't understand why the library allowed them to do so. Therefore, she took it upon herself to ask the couple why they needed to check out that many tapes at one time. They responded by telling her to "mind her own business." She then proceeded to inform them that it was extremely selfish to check out all those movies at once, because now those movies were unavailable to other patrons who might want them. She also decided to ask them, rather loudly in fact, if they were planning on hosting some type of 48 hour VHS watching orgy or something.

Jamie, the librarian on duty, decided at that time to intervene. He told Arianna to please be quiet, and that it was no concern of hers. Arianna responded by telling him that it WAS her concern, that as a tax-paying resident of Meadowville, she thought it was ridiculous that the library had no maximum limit set on how many VHS tapes, CDs or books the public could take out at one time. (Incidentally, the Meadowville Library still hasn't amended their lending policy, except now instead of allowing unlimited access to VHS tapes, it's DVDs. This still infuriates Arianna to this day, and, to their chagrin, she complains about it regularly to the librarians and the patrons.) She raised her voice and, according to Jamie, began yelling, "So, if I were to take a fricken shopping cart and roll it into the library, I could just dump every fricken book, VHS tape, and CD in here that I wanted to?!" That is when he decided she was seriously deranged and called the police.

Meanwhile, it was a very slow crime day in Meadowville, so policeman Mike Stevenson, he hadn't been the Chief back then, decided he'd be the one to respond to the call. It sounded like it might be a bit more exciting than the paperwork he was presently filling out for an arrest he had made the night before. When he arrived at the library, Arianna was screaming at Jamie the librarian, who looked like he was on the verge of tears.

"What seems to be the trouble here?" Mike asked. Arianna was only in her early twenties then, but was already showing signs of becoming the spitfire that she is today.

Instead of calming down when she saw a police officer, she became even madder. "Oh great, you HAD to go and call the coppers, didn't you!" she yelled at Jamie, who was now whimpering behind the desk.

Mike immediately thought she was really cute, and because she wouldn't shut up, he pretended that because of her unruliness, he was obliged to handcuff her. He also told her she was being taken back to the station to be put in a holding cell for disorderly conduct. Arianna was kicking and screaming all the way to the squad car. He pushed her gently into the backseat and slammed the door. Before he drove away, he looked over his right shoulder and asked, "Where do you live Miss Arianna Archer?"

"Why?" she warily replied.

"Because I'm going to take you home," he said.

She perked up. "Oh, you're not taking me to the station?"

"No, but I have a very serious question to ask you."

"Yes?" she answered, finally looking afraid.

"Do you have a boyfriend?"

She relaxed and smiled. "No, I don't," she answered. Arianna began to check him out and decided he wasn't that bad looking for a cop. After a couple of minutes of flirting, and Mike making her promise to stay away from the library for a week, they arranged a dinner date, and, as they say, the rest is history.

Mike had bowled with Arianna quite a few times over the years since then, and every single time, he would inevitably become frustrated and annoyed with her. Arianna loved bowling, almost as much as Mike did, but not only wasn't she very good at it, she didn't take it seriously at all. It never mattered to her who won or lost, and this effectively drove Mike nuts.

"But WHY don't you want to go bowling?" Arianna whined.

"Bowling with you is always aggravating, and besides, I don't think we should be playing with Sallie and Stanley," he replied.

"And why not?" she asked, with an irritated tone in her voice.

"Well, first of all, I don't want to have to watch a replay of last night's fiasco, and I would think you wouldn't want to either."

"Don't worry about that," she said, "I've already given her a stern talking to about drinking and her attire, but I'll have a talk with her about laying off all the lovey dovey stuff with Stanley too, just in case."

"Uh huh," he replied skeptically. "Also, something tells me that Sallie, just like certain OTHER people I know, will not take the sport seriously, and..."

She interrupted him, "Sport? You consider bowling a sport?"

"Of course I do," he answered. Arianna rolled her eyes. "But the biggest reason we shouldn't be bowling with them is, that I've been thinking about it, and regardless of his age, I don't think we should underestimate Stanley. If he is the killer, he could be dangerous," Mike said authoritatively.

"You have got to be kidding me! What do you think Stanley's going to do? Pour his Ex-Lax into your beer when you're not looking? The only way he could possibly hurt somebody, is if he got naked and grossed someone out so much that it caused them to shoot their own eyes out."

"Fine," Mike said evenly, "what time should I pick you up?"

"You know, if you've already made plans with Barbara, I'd understand," she said, again, spitting out his ex-wife's name as if it were poison.

"Riann...," he said in a tone that hinted he was just about to blow.

"Umm, 6:15 pm would be perfect, see you th..."

"Wait a minute, don't hang up," Mike interrupted. "I almost forgot to tell you, I have the results of the background checks on all the suspects," he informed her.

"Background checks?" Arianna asked, sounding worried.

"Yep, it's SOP to order one on anyone at the scene of a suspicious death who the police have cause to think might have something to do with it, but I ordered one on Arlene and Paula as well."

"SOP?"

"Standard Operating Procedure," he replied.

"Oh yeah, that's right. Did you uh, dig up anything on me?"

"No, I actually didn't feel the need to ask for one on you. Why? Is there something there to dig up?" he asked her suspiciously.

She breathed a sigh of relief. "Of course not," she replied defensively and quickly changed the subject. "So, did you find out anything interesting on any of the suspects?" she asked curiously.

"Yep, actually on two people. Stanley Carter was arrested about twenty years ago for solicitation of a prostitute."

"Figures," she said, "once a perve, always a perve. And the other person?"

"Your mother." He sighed, waiting for Arianna's inevitable overly dramatic reaction.

"My mother?! For what? Oh, don't tell me PROSTITUTION?!"

"No," even Mike had to laugh at that one, for it was very hard to imagine Sandra standing on a street corner, "she was arrested in a bar fight."

"A bar fight? There must be some mistake. Sandra Archer wouldn't be caught dead in a bar."

"Well, she was but don't worry, she didn't do any time for it."

"Do any time?" she repeated. Arianna was still reeling from shock. *Who is this woman?*

"Are you OK Riann?" he asked her, sounding concerned.

"I'm fine. Wait until Emily hears about this, it seems like Mother Dear has a lot of 'splainin' to do," she said, her face wrinkling into a frown. The doorbell rang. "Hang on a minute Mike, there's someone at the door," She walked over and looked through the peephole. "Well, speak of the devil herself, it's my mother. I'll have to call you back," she told him, and hung up before he could respond.

Arianna yanked her front door open. "Hey Mom, you want to explain to me why a criminal background check turned up an arrest on you for a bar fight?" she belligerently demanded.

"Well, what a nice way to welcome your mother, Ari..."

Arianna interrupted, speaking sharply to her, "Just answer the question!"

Sandra walked inside and stood next to the dining room table. "Oh that," she said, waving her hand dismissively. "Before I met your father, I was dating a delightful young man named Harold and he took me to a," she paused, "drinking establishment."

"You mean, a bar?" Arianna interjected.

"A drinking establishment," her mother said firmly. "We were there enjoying a lovely cocktail, when a large, uncouth burly man insulted me and Harold tried valiantly to defend my honor."

"This isn't the eighteenth century, Mother, men don't fight duels for ladies anymore!"

"May I finish?" Sandra asked sharply.

"Go on," Arianna said, sitting back on her sofa, her arms folded across her chest.

"But I could see that this buffoon was gaining the upper hand in the altercation. So I grabbed a bottle of wine from behind the bar and smashed it over his head, that's all. And then of course, the authorities were called, and there was this dreadful policeman, who I think actually took pleasure in upsetting me, and who insisted on arresting me. It's just too bad Michael wasn't around back then. It isn't like I killed the man or anything, Arianna," she defended herself. "Anyway, I was arrested for battery, but Harold managed to release me on bail and they threw the case out of court. So as you can see, I was merely trying to defend Harold." Arianna just sat there looking at her, mouth agape. "Please shut your mouth dear, you might accidentally swallow a flying insect."

"And you never thought to tell me this?"

"Why would I? What's done is done, you cannot change the past Arianna." She hated when her mother chose to state the obvious.

"What else have you been keeping from me all these years?" Arianna belligerently asked. Her face suddenly brightened. "Am I adopted?" she asked hopefully.

"Oh, don't be ridiculous," she told her.

Arianna's face fell and she stood up. "Mom, I need some time to process all of this, did you come over here with some particular reason in mind?"

"Yes, I did. I noticed you hadn't picked up the book yet that I ordered for you, so I generously decided to stop at the bookstore and pick it up for you." She walked over and handed her daughter the book.

Arianna took <u>Beggars Can't Be Choosers, a Guide for Single Women in Their Thirties</u> from her mother's hand and sighed. "Thank you Mother, was that it?"

"Yes dear, I'll be leaving now," she said, walking out the door. "Have a nice day."

"Too late for that," Arianna muttered, slamming the door shut behind her.

At 6:15 pm precisely, Mike beeped the horn and Arianna came walking out of the house, looking dazed. "So, did you have a talk with your mother?" he asked, as soon as she opened the passenger side door.

"I don't want to talk about it," she quietly answered. Mike didn't reply and decided to give her some space. Meadowville didn't have a bowling alley, and neither did any of the other nearby suburbs, so they had to drive about thirty-five minutes away to a town called Lakewood. Mike and Arianna arrived at the Chestnut Peaks Bowling Alley at 6:45 pm. Arianna had been silent the entire ride, but as soon as Mike parked the car, she turned to him and asked, "You're a cop, please tell me, is there any way I can legally divorce my mother?" Once again, forgetting that she asked Mike this question every time they watched <u>Nurse Jackie</u> together.

"Aww, just be glad you have one," he said, looking sad for a moment.

Arianna immediately felt bad. Mike and his mother always had a wonderful relationship. She was diagnosed with Alzheimer's about fifteen years ago and died five years later. Unfortunately, Arianna never knew Opal when she was vibrant and lucid, but she knew there wasn't a day that went by that Mike didn't think about her.

"I know, I'm sorry Mike," she said, as she touched his shoulder. "You lucked out when you got Opal as a mother."

He nodded and cleared his throat, "Yeah, I sure did.

Arianna was envious of Mike, for he was the oldest of four children, and had a great relationship with all of his siblings. His brother Matt lived close by in Somerset Hills and his sister Gloria lived right there in Meadowville. His other brother Dale lived in Indiana, so Mike didn't see him that much, but they all got together on Christmas Day every year. His family never interfered in Mike's personal life, even when he and Barbara were going through their divorce. Arianna couldn't ever remember a time when he complained about a family member. Conversely, she couldn't remember a time when she wasn't complaining about a family member.

They made their way through the huge parking lot over to the main door. Chestnut Peaks Bowling Alley was quite large. It contained a big restaurant/lounge area, which featured musical entertainment on Friday and Saturday nights, and a full bar. The prices were reasonable and the food, especially the pizza, surprisingly good. There were also arcade games off to the right side from where the shoe rental booth was located. Each lane contained a bunch of plush fluorescent green seats where the bowlers could sit and await their turn, and tables with cup holders to hold everyone's drinks and snacks. Above each lane there was a flashy neon pink screen which recorded and kept track of each of the players' scores. Every time a player would bowl a strike or a spare, the screen would light up and flash different bright colors, while loud pop music would start playing at the same time. Mike, who pretty much preferred everything old school, found this tacky and annoying. Arianna knew that if it were up to him, they'd all still be keeping score with paper and pencils.

Mike, as he always did when bowling, was wearing his lucky bowling shirt, which was black and yellow and had "Stevenson" in white embroidery on the back. He was carrying his very fancy-looking and expensive, gold-colored bowling ball and professional black bowling shoes. Arianna, on the other hand, was wearing dark blue sweatpants and a Chicago Cubs T-shirt. She planned, as usual, to just use the bowling alley's shoes and ball. Sallie and Stanley were already there on Lane 4, and Sallie was waving at them.

"Hi Riann!" Sallie greeted her with a hug. "Hi Mike!" To his surprise, she hugged him too. Arianna watched closely, just to make sure he wasn't enjoying the hug TOO much. Sallie was wearing hot pink bowling shoes with glittery red laces, a hot pink, glow-in the dark T-shirt and, what the young people call, "Daisy Dukes" (denim shorts that left little to the imagination). So much for taking it down a notch, Arianna thought resignedly. Stanley was wearing a white undershirt with brown suspenders and baggy brown pants. He brought his own bowling shoes, brown Oxfords, which looked like they had been through World War II. Taking into account how old Stanley was, they probably had, she thought.

"Hey Sallie," Arianna said, taking her off to the side, "can I talk to you for a second?"

"Sure, what's going on?" she said cheerfully.

"I hate to ask you this, but would you mind not being uhh, so physical with Stanley tonight while we're bowling."

"Why?" she asked, looking hurt, "I don't understand." Arianna cursed herself for, once again, not thinking ahead and coming up with a believable excuse ahead of time. Now she was obliged to think one up on the spot, which history had proven time and time again, was not something in which she excelled. Arianna was also forced to raise her voice because of all the noise in the background.

"Uhh, well, Mike has been a little depressed lately," she lied, thinking fast, "because it's been awhile since he's, uh, been able to perform in the bedroom." She lowered her voice while speaking the last few words.

"What? I can't hear what you're saying," complained Sallie.

Arianna looked around first to make sure Mike was far enough away not to overhear. "I said," she raised her voice, "Mike's been having problems performing in the bedroom lately." She looked down at her hands, as if she were ashamed, and sighed. "It's just work-related stress, you know. Seeing the worst of humanity day by day is, well, it's just been wreaking havoc on his manhood." Arianna managed to look as if she were about to cry at any second and was very proud of her performance. Arianna felt she could have easily been a dramatic actress, if just a few things had gone differently in her life. She often told her mother that if she'd only had the foresight to raise her in California, she would have been a famous actress by now.

"But I don't understand, I thought you said you two weren't dating right now?" said Sallie.

"Well, this is the primary reason why we aren't dating now," she explained, thinking fast. "This type of thing really screws up a relationship, you know. Anyway," Arianna continued, "I'm afraid he'll be jealous of Stanley, if he picks up on all the hot passion between you two. It may even make him more depressed," she explained, sadly shaking her head.

Sallie surprised Arianna, by swinging her arms around her and hugging her tightly. "Oh my God, really? Oh I'm SO sorry Riann! Of course, hands off, I promise! I TOTALLY understand, and if Mike ever wants to talk to Stanley, for you know, like some lovemaking tips or anything, just let me know." Arianna managed to squeak out a "thanks Sallie" before Sallie unleashed her chokehold on her. She went on, "Just know, we are here for you two!" Arianna, now totally self-conscious and paranoid someone might overhear them, was trying to get Sallie to stop talking, to no avail. "Or if you want to borrow some toys or books, or props, like handcuffs, or..." Fortunately, Arianna managed to drown out the sound of Sallie's voice, by thinking about her beloved Tony and Carmela, and wondering which room they would choose to spit up in, that evening.

Arianna was finally able to squeeze a word in edgewise and quickly excused herself to go find a ball. The bowling alley had a huge selection of bowling balls to choose from. Arianna usually used a thirteen or fourteen pound ball, depending upon her mood. The problem was, she had abnormally large fingers for a woman, (for which she blamed her Scandinavian heritage) and most of the balls at that weight did not have finger holes big enough to fit her. Consequently, it always took her way too long, in Mike's opinion anyway, to find a ball. However, tonight she lucked out and found a ball relatively quickly, so once she rented her shoes, the group was able to start their first game.

As the bowling got underway, as he expected, Mike's blood pressure soared. First of all, Sallie refused to put her fingers in the holes of her ball because she didn't want to mess up her nails. "Well, what is she supposed to do?" Arianna told him, when he expressed his dismay. "Do you know how much manicures cost?" Mike just groaned in response. Consequently, Sallie would grasp both sides of the ball, crouch down and throw the ball out from between her legs. This routine of hers gave all the men in the bowling alley quite the eyeful, yet predictably, did not result in the knocking down of many pins.

Arianna, on the other hand, would begin having a conversation with Mike or Sallie right before she was supposed to release the ball. Then, she wouldn't be paying attention to what she was doing, and she'd end up dropping the ball or accidentally whipping it in the next lane which, fortunately, in tonight's game did not result in any casualties. Also, whenever she'd do badly, which was almost always, she'd have some lame excuse ready. The excuses she used tonight were, in no particular order: the ball was too heavy; the ball was too light; it was too hot in the alley; her shoes were too tight; she was hungry; or Mike's particular favorite, she didn't have enough to drink. (Arianna believed her game was always better when she was slightly tipsy)

At the point where Mike was ready to kill himself, it was Stanley's turn. By the time Stanley got up off the chair, walked to the ball machine, picked up his ball and ambled up to the line, Arianna had time to use the washroom and come back. He would put his fingers in the ball, hold it in the correct position, and then drop it right into the gutter. He duplicated this on every single turn, and yet every time, Sallie would whoop and holler and say things like, "Good try sweetie pie!"

"I thought he was supposed to be some big bowling champ," Mike whispered to Arianna after Stanley's last turn.

"Yeah, but that was like in 1930 or something, maybe they had different balls or pins back then?" she suggested, shrugging her shoulders.

Mike sighed and rolled his eyes. "Oh, did you find out why Sarah and Rachel didn't come to Phil's wake?"

"Yeah, I called them both last night, right after I left. Sarah supposedly had the stomach flu or something, and Rachel, quote 'doesn't go to wakes or funerals' unquote," she replied in a disgusted tone of voice.

"Why do you sound so upset?"

"Oh, they were both annoyed that I called them and practically hung up on me," Arianna explained.

He rebuked her, "You could have waited until today to call them you know, Miss Impatient. You should have known better, you know how old people like to get to bed early."

"Yeah, yeah, yeah…"

"Hey, did you have a talk with Sallie about her public displays of affection?" he asked. "I noticed it hasn't been too bad tonight."

"Yep, everything's been taken care of," Arianna replied, with a fake smile plastered on her face.

"Glad to hear it," he said, and turned his attention back to the game.

Meanwhile, about every ten minutes, some man would walk past their lane, see Sallie, smile and call out, "Hi Sallie!" She'd respond by yelling, "Hi [Insert man's name here]!" and enthusiastically waving at them, effectively holding up the game.

Curious, Arianna asked Sallie, "How do you know all these men?"

"Shh!" she said, "I don't want Stanley to hear, but I've dated them."

"ALL of them?" asked Mike incredulously, scratching his head.

"Yes, but that's all in the past now. Stanley and I will be together forever." Arianna and Mike simultaneously made eye contact, knowing exactly what the other one was thinking about that.

At one point near the end of the game, both Arianna and Stanley were both using the restrooms, when Sallie walked over to Mike, put both hands on his shoulders, and shoved her face so close to his that they were almost touching noses. "Mike," she said, "Riann appreciates you for WHO YOU ARE! Remember that. You never have to prove anything to her."

Clearly perplexed and uncomfortable, Mike responded, "Um, OK?"

She took her hands off his shoulders, but continued to stare into his eyes. "You know, Riann is a very understanding woman."

"Yes, yes she is," he lied, playing along until he could figure out where this was going.

"Between you and me," she loudly whispered, "I don't think Riann's that much into sex anyway." She put a finger to her lips and walked stealthily away.

As soon as Arianna and Stanley got back, Mike asked Arianna in a very loud fake voice, "Riann, I'm going to get a beer, you wanna go with me?"

"Eh, not really, I'm..."

"Great, let's go!" Mike grabbed her left hand and pulled her over to the steps that led to the bar.

"Ouch! You're hurting me, I didn't want to go to the bar...," she complained.

"Be quiet. Listen, did you say something to Sallie about me?" he asked angrily.

"Say something to Sallie?" she repeated innocently, looking down at the floor, which to her dismay, was completely covered with gum and beer.

"You heard me."

"Um, I'm not sure, I've said lots of things to Sallie, I can't possibly remember them all," she replied with a guilty look on her face.

He crossed his arms over his chest. "Riann, while you were in the bathroom, Sallie said quite a few things to me, none of which make any sense. You wanna tell me what's going on?"

"Well," she said quietly, "I told Sallie to lay off the PDAs like you asked me to, being the good, dutiful woman that I am..."

"Riann, cut the bullshit, I'm in no mood," he warned her. "Bowling with you three tonight has been torturous."

"Oh, well alright, so you see, Sallie asked why I was asking her to lay off the PDAs. She looked so upset, like I had hurt her feelings, and I felt bad and I couldn't think of anything to say on the fly, so I...I," she stammered, "might have given her the impression that you were..." Arianna incoherently mumbled a bunch of words.

"I'm sorry," Mike said sarcastically, "I'm having trouble hearing you, please repeat that. You might have given her the impression that I was??"

"Having a hard time getting it up OK, so kill me!" she blurted out.

"WHAT?!" he cried out, quasi-ballistic. The tips of his ears had turned bright red, as well as his face.

She quickly apologized, "Listen Mike, I am so sorry. I told her that you had a lot of stress in your life recently. You know, cop stress," she explained, "and that you're really depressed about your, your um problem, and that being forced to witness their passionately hot relationship might make you even, you know, more depressed." She gave him a half-hearted smile.

"Why the hell would you tell her something like that?"

"I told you, that's the only thing I could come up with," she pleaded her case.

"Really Riann, you couldn't have just told her that I'm a prude, or that PDAs make me uncomfortable, or anything? Anything BUT that?!"

Arianna knew she'd better keep her mouth shut, but couldn't help herself. "Oh, who cares anyway, WE know the truth that you're really a big stud!" She gently elbowed him in the ribs. "Oh, I just remembered, Sallie MAY have offered Stanley up as someone who might have some, uh tips for you, in case you wanted to call on his expertise or anything…"

Mike shook his head. "Oh super, that's just great. Now this old coot is going to think he outperforms me!"

"Oh you men are sooo sensitive about your sexual prowess, it's ridiculous," she said, trying to make light of the situation, apparently to no avail, unfortunately. He stalked off and went back to join Sallie and Stanley. She felt miserable. *I'm sure Barbara, with all of her education and all, would have thought up something much better on the fly.* Arianna waited a couple of minutes before she joined them, wanting to give Mike a little time to cool off.

About twenty minutes later, after the first game was over, Mike announced the results, "Mike, 212, Arianna, 90, Sallie, 32, and Stanley, 4."

Sallie patted Stanley's arm, and in a cheerful voice said, "That's three whole pins better than last time, Honey."

"Well, good game everybody, I'm going to the bar," Mike said, and rapidly began walking away.

Arianna grabbed Mike's arm and whispered, "That's it, we're only playing one game?"

"Yes," Mike replied, as he sat down on one of the many barstools surrounding a well-stocked, noisy and crowded bar. "Bartender, pour me a double shot of whiskey," he ordered, motioning to the young, attractive woman tending the bar. He threw his keys to Arianna. "YOU'RE driving home tonight," he informed her.

Chapter Sixteen - Breakthrough

The next morning Arianna was in her bedroom sorting laundry. She felt it took way too much time and effort to fold everything, so after she'd sort everything into towel piles, sock piles, washcloth piles, etc., she'd grab each pile and just throw them into the appropriate drawer. Arianna was currently feeling annoyed and frustrated and believed they'd never find out the truth regarding Phil's death. Arianna was even debating whether or not she should just quit working on the investigation altogether. Her father John, used to always tell her to never give up, to finish what you start, and that the world hates a quitter. Because he held these values so dear, Arianna's freshman year in high school was an absolute, unequivocal hell.

Her mind flashbacked to autumn, 1992. Arianna, an antisocial freshman, who hated sports and all extracurricular activities in general, was talking with her best friend Susanne in the basement of Susanne's house. Susanne was determined to make the cheerleading squad and wanted Arianna to help her memorize a bunch of dance moves for tryouts. After much grumbling at first, Arianna begrudgingly agreed to help her out by repeating a lot of nonsensical arm and hand movements and one painful knee drop, which Susanne had choreographed, to the song "Jump Around" by House of Pain. Because the song was entitled, "Jump Around", Susanne also thought it would be a good idea, if during the last minute of the song, she jumped up and down like a pogo stick. Arianna secretly thought the routine was absolutely ridiculous, but faked her enthusiasm because she knew how much this meant to her friend. The day of the tryouts, Arianna was there with her in the Meadowville High School gym providing moral support, when Susanne turned to her and whispered, "Riann, everyone is trying out with partners. You have to be my partner!"

"What? You're crazy! I'm not going out there, I don't want to be a cheerleader!" she told her.

"Don't worry about it Riann, you're just there to be my partner. Do you seriously think they would pick you anyway?"

Arianna was too busy being nonplussed to feel insulted. "Well, then I'm going to look just absolutely stupid, it'll be way too embarrassing!"

"I said, don't worry about it. They'll see that you're just helping me out," Susanne assured her.

Arianna reluctantly went out there and, just as she expected, screwed up more than once. She was incredibly glad no one was videotaping the tryouts, for Arianna had the feeling that she and Susanne resembled a pair of Mexican jumping beans. Susanne; however, felt very optimistic about her chances. Arianna happened to be in the bathroom when the judges called out the names of the girls who made the squad. When she came out, Susanne was crying and told Arianna that she was never talking to her again.

To Arianna's shock and dismay, Susanne didn't make the squad, but Arianna did. She couldn't understand it, she had to be the worst cheerleader in the world, she was like the "Anti-Cheerleader". She found out months later, that they just needed a big tall girl to be one of the bottoms of their pyramid. Evidently, Susanne was four inches too short and twenty-five pounds too light. Arianna wanted to immediately resign of course, but her dad wouldn't let her. He told her, "Arianna, best finish what you start." Therefore, she was forced to be a cheerleader for the Meadowville High School cheerleading squad her entire freshman year.

It was absolute hell for Arianna, and from the get-go, it was pretty obvious that everybody hated her, including the coach. Arianna would always forget when the practices were scheduled, and one night she even forgot they had a game. She came in late in the middle of a routine and effectively ruined it for everyone. Arianna also couldn't remember half the moves she was supposed to make and never smiled;

thereby, consistently screwing up any hope of their squad ever winning a competition. She remembered constantly getting yelled at by their coach for not smiling. Arianna believed smiling was totally overrated, especially since she had horrible teeth. When posing for pictures, she would never open her mouth. Instead, she'd just crack a half smile with one side of her lips.

The last straw for the coach and the squad came at the biggest basketball game of the year. At the end of their pom pom routine, all the girls were waving their right hand in front of their stomachs, like they were strumming a guitar. Their gloves were green and white, and the green was supposed to be on the outside, the white on the inside. Arianna, of course, had accidentally put her gloves on backwards, and so when all the cheerleaders were waving with the green side, Arianna was smack in the middle of the line waving the white side. The coach and the other girls refused to even talk to her after that. You'd have thought she had killed somebody, the way they reacted. After this incident, she begged her father to let her quit, but he managed to make her feel so guilty, she stayed.

After that horrific experience, Arianna swore if she had any kids she'd tell them to give up anything they don't like doing, as soon as possible. She'd also teach them that there's no shame in quitting, and that if they wanted to be happy, they should quit as many things as possible. Therefore, Arianna had no qualms or misgivings about quitting the investigation. Her only misgiving about quitting was that she really did want to prove to Mike that she was a good and capable investigator.

Arianna's traumatic flashback was over, and she was running through the case in her mind, when suddenly, she recalled reading somewhere that people usually figure out the answer to a question or problem, when they drop it completely from their minds and think about something else instead. So she decided to settle down with an Agatha Christie and forget about the case for a while. She loved the Christie books which featured Hercule Poirot, but had read so many lately that she decided to go with a Miss Marple instead. Arianna was looking through her collection, trying to decide which Marple she was in a mood to read, when suddenly, her eyes widened. "Oh, it's a long shot of course, but maybe I'll get lucky," she said aloud. She ran to the living room to get her notebook out of her purse. She re-read all of the notes pertaining to the case that she had taken, and then sat at her computer for over an hour jotting things down. Next, she made a series of phone calls. Her first call was to Stanley Carter.

He finally answered on the ninth ring. "Hello?" he said in a shaky voice.

"Stanley, this is Arianna Archer." Having elicited no response, she added, "Sallie's friend? The one investigating Phil La Paglia's death?" Still silence. "I went bowling with you last night??"

"Ohhh yes, now I remember, you're the one whose boyfriend is having difficulty sustaining an erection. How can I help you?"

Arianna groaned. "Yep, that's me. Stanley, I just have one question to ask you." She told him, "It's concerning the women who covered the bar for you on the night of Phil's death."

He provided the information she requested. "Anything else, my dear?"

"No Stanley, thank you, you've been very helpful," she cheerfully replied.

Her next call was to Mike. Sounding rushed, she asked him, "Mike, is it too late for the medical examiner to check Phil's blood for something specific? Would he need to exhume the body?"

"Not necessarily," he replied, "I'm pretty sure in cases when the cause of death is unknown, he collects a clean blood sample before he releases the body to the family, but I'll double-check. Why do you ask?"

"Can you please call in a favor and have him run a test for...," she said, naming the substance. "It's very important we get the results ASAP. I'll explain everything later."

"Will do," he promised. "Oh, I almost forgot, let me quickly give you the scoop on Stanley's finances." He gave her an overview of what he discovered.

"Hmm, interesting," she replied.

"I also looked into the reason Camille got fired, like you asked." Mike proceeded to tell her what he learned.

"Very interesting, thanks Mike."

"I'll call you as soon as I have any information on the test," he promised. "It won't be for several hours though, at least," he added and hung up.

Arianna ended up staying home all day and doing a lot of research on the web. She had made several more phone calls, her excitement growing after each one. Many hours later, Mike called her back, right as she was just about to lose her mind with anticipation. "Hey doll, it's me," Mike said. "It was an easy enough test, they took the vial of uncontaminated blood that they had kept aside and yes, you'll be happy to know it tested positive for what you hoped. This is huge Riann, great job!"

"Awesome, thanks! I have a theory that's developing," she said brimming with enthusiasm. Arianna told him everything she discovered and what she suspected. She laid everything out as clearly as possible. "Well, what do you think?" she asked him, literally with bated breath.

"Well," he drew out the words slowly, "you may have a case here, but unless we can get a warrant and see what my men can find there, we definitely don't have enough evidence to make an arrest." Arianna made a disappointed sound in reply. "Let me call Judge Hawkins tomorrow morning though. It should be a piece of cake to get a warrant, he and I are old friends."

"Who aren't you old friends with?" Arianna rhetorically asked with admiration.

A little bit later, Arianna looked at the clock. *Wow, it is super late. Time flies when you're solving a murder, I guess.* She didn't even realize she hadn't eaten dinner, but surprisingly for her, food was the last thing on her mind. Arianna was just so excited, that she had a lot of trouble sleeping. She debated whether or not to call Mike and request that he bore her to sleep by talking about football or some other lame subject, but decided he might get annoyed. Mike tended to get upset at the littlest things, she reminded herself, recalling the whole "impotence" incident on their recent double date. She knew she was putting him through a lot lately; therefore, she decided it was best not to risk it. Instead, she debated reading something until she fell asleep. She picked up the book on her nightstand that her mother had bought her, read the back cover, and then tossed it into her garbage can. Arianna ended up watching late night television instead into the wee hours of the morning.

When she woke up, she could hardly believe it, it was already 10:30 am. It seemed like she had just laid her head down on her pillow. She gave a wide yawn and then went to fix herself some breakfast. Arianna hardly had any appetite, and so she barely finished a half of an English muffin with cherry jelly and a small glass of orange juice.

Her cell phone buzzed and when she saw it was Mike, she answered immediately, dying from anticipation. "Hello, what happened, did you get the warrant?"

"Yes, we did, luckily for us the judge is an early riser."

"Awesome!"

"After I talked to you last night, I called Ed and told him about the progress we've made. Needless to say, he is very pleased. He allowed me to put a couple men on the suspect's home this morning and as soon as the suspect is safely out of there, they will go in there and make their search."

"Great!" she replied, "regardless of what they find though, I'm gathering everybody at the church tonight at 6:00 pm. Please be there and, of course, bring backup, just in case."

"Roger that," he replied and disconnected.

Afterwards, she quickly got dressed. Luckily, Mike was able to score her an official policeman's light blue shirt and navy blue pants, which she had requested a couple of days ago. As instructed, he had left it in a bag on her doorstep late last night, after his shift. To Arianna's disappointment, he had balked at procuring her a badge or gun, but she was trying not to let that bother her too much. Even with her rapidly increasing girth, the uniform was still about two sizes too big, so she was forced to wear a big black belt and fasten it on the tightest hole. She also put on a pair of clunky black shoes that went quite well with the rest of the ensemble. This time though, unlike the day they visited Arlene, she wore her hair down and put on some makeup, just in case Mike was right and someone did mistake her for a lesbian.

She made a call to Sarah Brewster. It went straight to voice mail, so Arianna left a message. "Hello Sarah, it's Arianna Archer, can you please come to St. Francis this evening at 6:00 pm, and bring Esther, Camille and Rachel with you. It's in regard to some new developments in the inquiry into Phil La Paglia's death, and it is imperative that everyone be there. Thank you."

She then called Arlene, who was extremely curious when Arianna invited her to the meeting requesting that she bring Paula with her. Arianna firmly told Arlene that she couldn't give her any information at this time, but that later, all would be revealed. Lastly, Arianna contacted Sallie and asked her to bring Stanley and Sandra to the church that evening.

"Oh sure, but why?"

"I'll explain everything tonight, but I believe I've, we've cracked the case," she told her confidently.

"What? Really! Oh tell m…"

She cut her off. "Sorry Sallie, I've got to go, I have a lot of things I need to do before then."

"OK," she replied, obviously more than a little disappointed.

"See you later," Arianna said as she closed the phone.

She arrived at the church about twenty minutes early, that evening, to set some chairs up, and basically just paced back and forth for a while, until her guests arrived. Luckily, she had thought to call one of the pastors at St. Francis that afternoon, and asked that he leave the basement door unlocked. He readily agreed, especially when told she was holding a meeting regarding the investigation into Phil La Paglia's death. His reaction was not surprising, since Arianna had heard church attendance had taken a nosedive since the unfortunate event.

Surprisingly, Stanley Carter was the first to turn up, accompanied by Sallie Rigelli, who was wearing a black one-piece, skin-tight latex suit, which made her without a doubt, the sexiest Catwoman ever, and Sandra Archer, who was revealing more skin than Arianna had ever seen in her life. (Arianna never asked, but just assumed she was never breast-fed, for she was fairly certain her mother would consider breast-feeding a bit too unseemly) Sandra was sporting a silver mini-skirt paired with a filmy, extremely low-cut, red blouse, and very high, red spiked heels. *Oh my God, is she wearing a push-up bra?!* What has Sallie done to my mother? she worried. Sandra Archer was accompanied by a strange man, who was wearing aviator sunglasses, gold medallions around his neck, a mustache, bad *toupee*, and a "Smokey and the Bandit" like red jumpsuit, which revealed tons of dark brown chest hair. He cracked his gum loudly, to Arianna's dismay.

Sandra introduced them to each other. "Hello Arianna, this is Barry Richards. Barry, this is my daughter Arianna."

"Hey how YOU doin?" he said, just like the character "Joey" on the hit TV show, Friends.

She took a step back, as he was dangerously close to invading her personal space. "Uhh, are you a Burt Reynolds impersonator or something?" she asked, trying to avoid looking at his chest hair.

"No, I'm not honey, but I do get asked that question a lot. Me and Burt gots lots of similarities."

Arianna flashed him a fake smile and then pulled Sandra off to the side. "Where the hell did you find Burt?"

Sandra Archer looked her daughter up and down. "I found him on Facebook. His name is *Barry*, and I would appreciate it if you would treat him nicely."

"Yeah, well 1975 called, they want their porn star mustache back," she told her snidely.

"Well, at least HE doesn't look like a lesbian." Her mother stalked off and made her way back to Barry, putting her hand on his shoulder, solely for her oldest daughter's benefit.

Arianna whined, "But I wore makeup and everything!"

Sallie came over and grabbing her arm with excitement, said to Arianna, "Quick, before everyone else gets here, tell me who did it!"

"I'm sorry, but I'm not going to tell you anything, Sallie. It'll be more fun for you, if you're surprised like everyone else," explained Arianna.

Sallie frowned and dejectedly responded, "Okay, I understand." She walked back over to Stanley, very disappointed.

A few minutes later, Arlene and Paula arrived, shortly followed by Sarah, Rachel, Camille, and Esther. Seeing the mother and daughter side by side, only served to highlight the extreme differences between them. Arlene was wearing a pale pink, freshly ironed summer dress with matching *espadrilles* and small white hoop earrings, which perfectly complemented her blonde and auburn hair. Arlene's frosted pink lipstick also matched her long, beautifully manicured fingernails. While Paula, on the other hand, was wearing giant, baggy shorts and a stained, violet-colored, short-sleeved shirt. Her hair was looking just as greasy and lifeless, as the first time Arianna met her. She also wore dirty white tennis shoes with no socks, and it appeared as if her legs hadn't seen a razor in months.

However, it appeared as if all of the women were staring at Sallie and Stanley, not Arlene and Paula. The two lovebirds were standing off to the side, holding hands and whispering to each other. As soon as Esther realized Sallie and Stanley were a couple, if looks could kill, the pair would definitely be six feet under by now.

Arianna imperiously commanded everyone to take a seat, motioning towards the straight line of chairs, which she had set up earlier on the basement floor. Everyone quickly grabbed a seat and, within a minute, the room was so quiet you could hear a pin drop.

Since Mike wouldn't give her a gun, wishing to look like a genuine policewoman, Arianna had brought with her a policeman's baton novelty item, a prop for an old Halloween costume, which she had found in the back of her closet. She began the proceedings by swinging it around, as she walked back and forth in front of the suspects. "Thank you all for coming. I asked you here today, because you all are either related to Phil La Paglia or you were right here in this basement the night he died. The Meadowville Chief of Police, Mike Stevenson had asked me…"

Interrupting her, Sallie loudly whispered to everyone, "Riann's boyfriend." Most of them remarked, "Oh," not really caring, but nodding in response anyway.

Arianna paused. "He is NOT my boyfriend," she emphatically stated. Looking mildly exasperated, she continued, "As I was saying, Chief Stevenson asked me to be a consultant on an inquiry into Phil's death, after the cause of death appeared to be coming up inconclusive. The medical examiner and the police had no idea if he died from natural causes, an accidental overdose, suicide or murder. His personal doctor informed the police that Phil was in excellent condition with no history of seizures or convulsions, so natural causes were beginning to look less likely. An accident would indicate a willingness on Phil's part to ingest a drug of some sort. We quickly determined he wasn't the type to take illegal drugs; however, he was tested for as many illegal and prescription drugs as possible, and the toxicology reports came up negative. He was taking absolutely no drugs or medications."

Stanley piped up, "I take twenty-four!" Everyone turned to look at him and then quickly went back to focusing on Arianna.

"After hearing about what kind of man Phil was, I ruled out suicide right away. According to all accounts, Phil very much enjoyed living, and even if he were to take his own life, I was pretty sure he'd be considerate enough not to do it in front of a room full of ladies, or at a church, no less. Since everything else was basically eliminated, the only explanation left was murder by some type of poison. Mike informed me that Phil's tox screen had also come up negative for arsenic, cyanide and strychnine. So how exactly did he die, I asked myself."

"Yesterday morning, I was contemplating which Agatha Christie mystery I wanted to read, and I was suddenly struck with an idea. Christie features many types of poisons in her books. In fact, poison was her favorite method of murder in her writings. I remembered that in two of her books, she had used one poison in particular. In this investigation, I hadn't heard anyone mention this specific poison as a possible means of murdering Phil. I was optimistic though that if they tested for this poison, they would find it in Phil's bloodstream. The poison that I am specifically referring to is Belladonna." At this point, the suspects all turned to look at one another with puzzled expressions on their faces.

I remembered that the symptoms Phil experienced the night he died were: dilated pupils, light sensitivity, loss of balance, hallucinations, and convulsions. All of these just happen to be the exact symptoms of Belladonna poisoning. I told Mike Stevenson to ask the medical examiner to do a test for Belladonna on the clean sample of Phil's blood, which was taken before he officially released the body. Sure enough, it came up positive, and the medical examiner verified that Phil La Paglia did indeed die from Belladonna poisoning." Arianna stopped speaking, and noticed them all staring at her, mouths wide open.

Sallie interjected, "But what's a Belladonna?"

Arianna smiled and answered, "It's a plant Sallie. *Bella Donna* actually means 'beautiful lady' in Italian, but the juice from the Belladonna plant's berries are dangerously lethal. All it takes is five berries to kill a grown man. We don't hear about this deadly nightshade hardly at all anymore. At one time though, Belladonna was quite popular. Women even put it in their eyes in order to dilate their pupils, believing for some odd reason, that this made them look sexier. The harmless parts of the plant are actually prescribed today for a host of gastrointestinal disorders. Belladonna is not native to the United States, but like most things nowadays, it's surprisingly easy to order off the Internet. I will expound on this subject a little later."

"Now that I had established what Phil died of, I needed to figure out exactly how the killer poisoned Phil. I never believed that the killer slipped something into Phil's glass. This would have been extremely difficult, for the killer would have almost certainly been seen by someone. After thinking about it for a while, I realized that the murderer didn't necessarily have to obtain access to the liquor cabinet keys and then drop the poison into the Jim Beam bottle, Phil's known drink of choice, which had been my original theory. It dawned on me that Stanley Carter took enough bathroom breaks that night, that anyone who covered for him as bartender, could have easily switched the bottles of JB out with one that contained the poison. While subbing for Stanley, any woman with a large enough bag or purse could do it easily without anyone noticing. The first time she subbed for him, she could set her purse down behind the bar and quickly make the exchange. Then later, when the killer covered for him again, exchange the bottles back. The killer knew that the dances were primarily attended by women who would never order JB, so I'm guessing she wouldn't be all that worried that someone else could possibly be poisoned as well. However, I'm hoping that she would have had at least the integrity to have quickly intervened if someone else ordered the bourbon first."

Arianna stopped pacing back and forth and stood still for a moment. "Although I didn't know for sure, I was pretty confident that this was how Phil was poisoned. Next, I turned to looking at who could have possibly killed him. The first person Mike and I interviewed was Arlene La Paglia." She stopped in front of Arlene. "A woman who, according to her, had a very amicable divorce with Phil, which she supposedly initiated. I asked Chief Stevenson to inquire into this, and by all accounts, we have no reason not to believe her. Therefore, I wondered, what probable reason could she have for killing Phil? If we look at a possible financial motive, it appears as if Arlene was living quite comfortably. However, we soon discovered she had lost most of her money when the market crashed a few years ago." Arlene, embarrassed, looked down at her hands. "Phil died without a life insurance policy or a will though, and this put all his money into their daughter Paula's hands, not hers. I actually believe Arlene would have had more of a chance to get some of Phil's money if he were still alive."

Arlene spoke up proudly, "I would never ask Phil for money, but if I did, there's no doubt in my mind he would have given me anything I'd ask for."

Arianna nodded and said, "Yes, I'd have to agree." She resumed her pacing again, then stopped in front of Paula. "I turned my focus next to Paula La Paglia. She admits there wasn't any love lost between her and Phil, but Paula was being supported by both parents financially. I honestly did not see enough hate, or passionate feelings of any kind, for that matter, to justify the murder of her own father. Yes, she now inherits his money, but after visiting with her, I quickly determined that she was not the money-grubbing type." Sallie nodded her head vigorously. Arianna noticed and said, "Oh, by the way, Sallie Rigelli also helped me with this investigation, and I'd be remiss if I didn't take a moment to thank her. Thank you Sallie." Everyone turned to look at Sallie, who was sitting there beaming and nudging Stanley with her elbow.

Arianna took a few steps forward. Now standing in front of Stanley, she continued, "Now, let's consider Stanley Carter for a moment. It appeared as if he had barely known Phil, so it was hard to imagine any possible motive there at first. However, Sallie had let me know privately that she had just learned that Stanley was actually Phil La Paglia's biological father." Like any good actress would, she paused for dramatic effect, and the room did not disappoint her. All of them gasped collectively. "It turns out Stanley over here," she pointed at him with her baton, "had a hard time keeping it in his pants back then." Everyone looked at him with shocked expressions, while he turned red in the face. "However, nobody besides Stanley and Phil's mother, Carol knew this, not even Phil himself, until just a week or so ago when he divulged his secret to Sallie. Chief Mike Stevenson inquired into the state of Stanley's finances. He's not rich, but he's doing fine with his plumber union's pension checks and Social Security payments. It doesn't really matter; however, because he doesn't stand to gain anything by Phil's death. Parents don't factor into the equation of inheritance when the deceased doesn't leave a will. Besides he's, let's just say, up there in age. Even if there was a financial motive, Stanley has to know he could kick the bucket at any moment, so why go to all the trouble to kill someone, when he's probably not going to be alive long enough to reap the benefits?"

At this point, Stanley, with an annoyed look on his face, cried out, "Hey!" Sallie patted his arm reassuringly while Arianna, not surprisingly, just ignored his outburst.

In the meantime, Arlene had become quite emotional and poked Paula in the arm, telling her, "You have a grandfather Paula." Paula who, for once appeared as something besides apathetic, mumbled something in return which Arianna couldn't overhear, despite her exceptional hearing. Arianna was born with horrific eyesight and forced to wear glasses at a very young age, but possibly to compensate for her quasi-blindness, she was gifted with exceptional hearing. In her experience, she found that quite often this gift came in handy, especially in regards to office gossip.

Arianna walked over to Camille. "In considering another suspect, Camille Ciccone, Mike and I learned that her family and Phil La Paglia's family had a feud many many years ago back in Sicily. Two young men, one from each family, had fought over a woman. One shoved the other and sadly, he ended up hitting his head and dying. This caused a very volatile feud between the families for decades; a real vendetta," Arianna informed them.

"Those hot-blooded Italians, what tempers they have!" Sandra loudly whispered to Barry, forgetting that Sallie was half Italian. However, Sallie didn't appear to be insulted and Camille just sat there looking rather bored.

Arianna continued her story, "However, we discovered the families had patched things up years ago, so her possible motive appeared to evaporate."

"Next, I took a look at Sarah Brewster." Arianna paused at Sarah's chair. "Sarah didn't seem to have anything personal against Phil, but then we learned that her husband Steve had actually been business rivals with him. Phil was much more successful than Steve; thereby, taking most of his business away. Consequently, Steve was forced to sell his business and retire early. Now perhaps, Sarah on some vendetta on behalf of her husband, could have decided to kill Phil. There were rumors that Steve was very upset at the time. However, Steve sadly ended up passing from lung cancer, and as Sarah told me, if he hadn't retired early, she and her husband wouldn't have had the little time they did have, to spend together. Therefore, the fact that Steve had been forced to retire early was actually a kind of a blessing in disguise." Arianna looked over at Sarah who, appearing a little sad, slowly nodded.

Arianna moved on, lingering in front of Rachel. "OK, let's consider Rachel Gordon for a moment. Phil accidentally rear-ended her a few years ago, and had been making monthly payments to her, supposedly out of guilt and the kindness of his heart. Her injuries didn't appear to be that serious, but it seemed to me after observing her, that Rachel was a lot more hurt than she had led everyone to believe. I wondered if she might have killed him out of anger for all the physical suffering she had endured." Rachel appeared startled, while everyone else looked dubious. "However, because of Phil dying, her payments ceased. So really, what good would Phil's death do her?"

Arianna made her way over to Sandra's chair and stopped. "My mother, Sandra Archer was there at the dance the night Phil died, but I never considered her a serious suspect. She barely knew Phil, and knowing my mother very well," she paused for a second, then resumed speaking, "um, let's just say, pretty well." She shot her mother a disgusted look. "I know she would consider killing someone quite bad manners, or at least a serious social *faux pas*." Sandra nodded her head in agreement. "Murder would be much more serious than, let's say a bar fight, for example, wouldn't you agree?" She looked pointedly at her mother, who gave Arianna an offended look in return.

"Which brings me finally to Esther Sullivan." Arianna stood in front of Esther and spun her baton. We all know about her turbulent divorce and her rage against her ex-husband. We also witnessed her recent over-the-top distaste for men in general, especially those who court young hot babes. But would she really go so far as to kill Phil for that? I would have to say 'no'. Why risk everything she did have, which seems to be a lot, judging by her fancy condo. If she really did feel this uncontrollable rage and hatred towards all men, wouldn't she have already gone on some killing spree and murdered all the middle-aged men who dated, cheated with or married younger women that she could? No, her rage was pretty much all focused on her ex-husband and he's still alive." Esther folded her arms across her chest and rolled her eyes.

Sallie spoke up, "Then is Phil's killer, someone who's NOT here? Nobody here seems to have a good motive for murder," she explained in a confused voice.

"Patience, Grasshopper," Arianna said softly, talking to Sallie as if she were a child. She seemed to be ignoring the fact that if Mike were there, he'd be thinking that if there was anyone in the world who should NOT be telling others to be patient, it was Arianna. "Someone here is indeed a murderer, I just haven't touched upon the correct motive yet." Everyone was now appearing quite jittery and looking at each other suspiciously.

"We ended up getting lucky though. One great turning point in the investigation was when Sarah told Sallie and me that the day Phil died, he was extremely worried about someone. So worried in fact, that he was asking Sarah for advice on what to do about it." The room grew eerily quiet, with all eyes focused on Arianna. "He told her that he had tried to terminate some kind of relationship with this person, but it had not turned out well. Phil didn't specify whether or not this was a friend, relative, work colleague or lover, nor did he give any clues as to who this person was. However, the motive for murder it has been said many times, is almost always love or money. In this particular case; however, I started playing with the idea of the motive perhaps being crazed obsession."

"I knew it!" Sallie cried, glaring at Esther, who frowned back at her.

"By all accounts, Phil was exceptionally nice, considerate and generous. This made it very difficult for me to imagine why anybody would want to kill him. However, it popped into my head that Phil was also handsome, charming, and well-off, and it would not be inconceivable that somebody could harbor an unhealthy type of obsession with him, but I'll revisit this in a few minutes. So to recap, I had already figured out what the cause of death was and how the murder was accomplished. I was now concentrating on who committed this deadly crime and why. I had pretty much eliminated Stanley from our pool of suspects, not only because he's older than dirt and slower than molasses on a cold January morning, but everyone who has read any Agatha Christie mysteries, knows that poisoning is almost always a woman's crime."

"Yay!" Sallie clapped her hands, then gave Stanley a hug, who at this point was pretty much unresponsive. Stanley was beginning to have trouble keeping his eyes open, as it was fast approaching the last of his many daily naptimes.

"I also knew that Belladonna poisoning works very fast, which meant that Phil had to have been poisoned at the dance. Phil arrived at the dance at approximately 7:30 pm and began experiencing symptoms around 9:15 pm. Therefore, Arlene and Paula were automatically excluded from being Phil's killer." Arianna quickly glanced over at Arlene, who had been listening intently and appeared visibly relieved.

"Stanley told me that Esther, Camille and Rachel covered for him at the bar that night. Sarah was too preoccupied tending to other details pertaining to the dance. Because of my theory of how the poison was administered to Phil, my suspect list was now narrowed down to four ladies, Sarah, who always had access to the liquor cabinet because she had a set of keys, Esther, Camille, and Rachel, who all subbed as bartender for Stanley that evening.

"Oh how ridiculous!" Esther cried, crossing and uncrossing her legs nervously.

"Let her finish," Sarah told her sternly. Esther shut her mouth, silently glaring at Arianna during the rest of the proceedings.

"Thank you Sarah," Arianna said, and went on speaking. "Looking at the four women who remained as suspects, I quickly crossed Sarah off the list. It was obvious that she had a long happy marriage with her late husband, and that her life was quite full with her daughters and grandchildren now. I couldn't picture her as someone who would be consumed with a man period, let alone be crazily obsessed with a man and kill him. She seemed much too grounded for that."

Suddenly, Arianna heard a noise behind her and ceased talking. Chief Mike Stevenson had arrived in his police uniform and was holding up a big brown paper bag.

Arianna frowned. She was pretty upset with Mike for not being there at 6:00, like she had asked. "Well, how nice of you to join us Chief Stevenson. What happened, did someone drop by and make you late? Perhaps, someone like Barbara??"

"Better late than never," he responded cheerfully.

"Who's Barbara?" Sandra whispered to Sallie. Sallie shrugged her shoulders.

"Excuse me," Arianna told everyone, "I'd like to request a sidebar with Chief Stevenson here. Let's take a five minute recess." She grabbed Mike's hand and led him into a small room off of the basement and closed the door.

As soon as the door was shut, Mike said, "You've been watching WAY too much Court TV."

"Hush, you're late!" she reprimanded him.

"Well, I had good reason to be late, Miss Archer," he replied, pointing to the paper bag.

"Hmmm, what do we have here?" she asked. He handed her the bag. She peered inside and withdrew its contents. "Wow," she exclaimed looking at Mike, "this is fantastic!"

"I thought you'd be pleased," Mike replied proudly, with a grin.

After a brief discussion, ten minutes later, Arianna and Mike walked back into the center of the basement. Everyone was out of their seats and walking around chatting nervously, except for Stanley, who was fast asleep, and Barry, who was surreptitiously trying to adjust his *toupee*.

Sandra waved her hand, motioning to Arianna to come closer. "Can we please get on with it dear? Barry and I do have plans tonight." *Yuck, I can't even imagine what kind of plans THEY have.* It's probably better not to, she quickly decided.

"Attention!" Arianna yelled. "Please, everyone sit down, court is now back in session." They all looked at her quizzically, while Mike gave a great sigh and made himself comfortable.

Arianna turned around quickly, swinging her baton and hitting her own arm in the process. "Ow!" she cried, blushing. She rubbed her arm and continued, "The police ascertained from Phil's GPS that he had visited two women on the day of his death, Rachel and Sarah. Rachel told us he came by to drop off one of his monthly payment checks, which he had been giving her since the traffic accident. According to her, they chit-chatted for twenty minutes about nothing in particular, but how do we know this is true?"

"Now, as I mentioned before, Sarah says Phil came over specifically to ask her for advice about a person in his life who was troubling him. Sarah told us she didn't even know if it was a man or a woman, but can we really trust her? As Sallie, so intelligently remarked, 'Maybe she's making the whole thing up to throw suspicion away from herself?' How do we really know?"

"As if I would do such a thing!" Sarah said with dignity.

Arianna glanced over at Mike, who wasn't looking at Arianna, but preoccupied watching one suspect in particular. "Now, one thing I've learned in my years of solving mysteries…"

"Actually, it is year, singular," Sandra loudly whispered to Barry.

Arianna gave her a dirty look and raising her voice a little louder, continued. "One thing I've learned is to always trust your gut or intuition," she said, while walking past the three ladies. Esther deftly ducked as Arianna just barely missed hitting her in the face with the baton. Arianna explained, "Agatha Christie's heroine, Jane Marple, was able to solve so many murders because she had already been familiar with the worst of human nature within the little village in which she lived. The guilty suspect would remind her of someone she once knew in St. Mary Mead, who would happen to be a thief, a blackmailer, or even perhaps, a murderer."

"I had commented to Chief Stevenson that one of the suspects kept reminding me of Cassie Rogers, a high school classmate of mine, who had actually been obsessed with me. This kind of gnawed at me because the two really looked nothing alike, and I couldn't figure out why I kept thinking there was a resemblance. However, yesterday I realized that they both shared the same type of blank dead look or facial expression. In order to hide her obsessive feelings towards me, Cassie would adopt this blank look every time she'd see me. I always thought she was strange and never really liked her, but when she began asking me to go to the mall with her, I'd go. However, she soon became very possessive. She didn't want me talking to anyone else and actually called a boy I was dating at the time, and threatened him, telling him, he'd better stay away from me, because he wasn't good enough for me. I didn't find this out until much later. She'd become angry if I called anyone else, or if she saw me hanging out with other girls. She also called me so much that my parents began suspecting she had a problem. Remember Mom?"

"Oh, yes," Sandra replied, nodding, "she was quite the nut job."

"When I realized how crazy she was, I severed our friendship in the nicest way possible, but she became insanely angry and wrote me a nine page letter filled with profanity and threats of bodily harm. That letter was actually pretty scary. If that happened nowadays, I'd probably take out a restraining order against her. Unfortunately, I spent most of the second half of my junior year preoccupied with figuring out ways to avoid her."

Arianna stopped walking, and with an extremely serious expression on her face, deliberately looked at each and every one of the suspects. "You know, Esther Sullivan's feelings were very apparent, they were right in your face, but the woman I'm speaking of, her feelings were not. I thought about this suspect and asked myself, if perhaps she could have some hidden obsession like Cassie. I had noticed while in the bathroom at Phil's wake, that this person was scrubbing her hands over and over, so hard I thought her skin would start peeling off. I easily recognized obvious obsessive-compulsive behavior, so it didn't seem that far-fetched to me that this woman could have a serious screw loose. The woman who reminded me of Cassie Rogers is," Arianna stopped in front of the suspect's chair, gave a long dramatic pause, then said, "Camille." Everyone gasped and with shocked expressions on their faces, slowly turned to look at her.

"While interviewing her, Camille told me she recently did some secretarial work for a project she was collaborating on with Phil. Sallie and I called her last place of employment and discovered that Camille's former boss had some 'personal issues' with her. I asked Mike to look into it, and apparently, she had developed an obsession with her former boss. Luckily, he had nipped it in the bud early on and fired her. Ironically, she was an exemplary employee and her work was excellent, so it was all hushed up to prevent Camille from suffering any embarrassment. I also remembered noticing Camille's extensive Agatha Christie collection while I was in her apartment. That proved to me that she was familiar enough with the deadly effects of Belladonna since Dame Agatha used that specific method of murder in The Caribbean Mystery and The Big Four. You see, Camille owned both books."

Camille stood up and raised her voice, "I don't have to listen to this nonsense!"

Mike barked, in a no-nonsense tone, "Sit down!" and a few seconds later, albeit with a nasty look at Arianna, she complied.

"You know, murder is easy," Arianna told the room, while swinging her baton again. "There's even a book by Christie titled, Murder is Easy, but it's the actual getting away with it that's hard. Yesterday, I found the top ten sites on the Internet, which sell the Belladonna plant and called each of them, pretending like I wanted to purchase the deadly nightshade. However, I also told them that I didn't want to potentially duplicate the order of my roommate, Camille Ciccone, who was on vacation. I further explained that I didn't want to disturb her and possibly ruin her vacation, so I asked if they could first look and see if my roommate had already placed an order. The first four companies told me they had no record of Camille purchasing any plants, but luckily, on the fifth place I called, I got a hit."

"I also called Stanley yesterday, and he told me that all three of the women who covered as bartender for him, worked the bar twice. Two of the three women, Stanley had to ask to sub for him, but only one woman actually VOLUNTEERED both times. Why don't you tell everyone who that was Stanley?" Everyone turned their rapt attention to Stanley, (who fortunately, was awake at the moment) who slowly raised his hand and shakily pointed his arthritic finger at Camille. They all began whispering in hushed tones to one another, while continuing to stare at Camille.

"None of this proves anything," Camille responded scornfully.

"Maybe not, but combined with the confirmation by the Internet company that you had ordered the Belladonna from them, it constituted enough evidence for a judge to issue a warrant to search your apartment. The police found some interesting emails on your computer today, Camille. Emails you sent to Phil and his replies back to you, which reflected not only your sick obsession with him, but his very clear disinterest in you!" In her excitement, Arianna spun her baton even faster, and it suddenly flew out of her hands and sailed across the room, nearly hitting Stanley in the head. Mike went over and picked up the baton, wisely keeping it on his person for the rest of the proceedings.

"Let's read the emails, shall we?" said Arianna. She walked over to Mike and he handed her the evidence bag. She pulled out a small stack of papers and read aloud the following:

April 26, 2014

My Dearest Phil-

I have loved you with all of my being since day one of working on this project with you. You mean everything to me. Please, let's leave and go somewhere away together soon.

Your Ever Faithful, Camille

May 1, 2014

Camille-

I'm so sorry if I led you on in any way, but I am not interested in any kind of relationship with you. You are a lovely lady, but I am only interested in working on this project together.

Phil

May 3, 2014

Dearest Phil-

You say that, but I know you don't mean it. Anyone can see the chemistry we have together, for we make the perfect couple. I think of you all day and all night long, and cannot wait until Tuesday when we shall see each together again.

Camille

May 8, 2014

Camille-

I think it's best to sever our work together on this project. I spoke to my colleague Brendan, and he assures me he can take over from here. Thank you for the fine job you've done. Enclosed is a check for the work you've already finished.

Regards, Phil

May 9, 2014

Mr. La Paglia-

I see, well thank you for letting me know. Good luck with your project.

Camille Ciccone

Arianna looked up from the papers she was reading from. "That last e-mail to Phil makes it look like Camille was okay with him having spurned her advances and firing her from his project. However," she paused, pulling out another piece of paper from the bag, "this reduced-size copy of a giant photograph of Phil, found by the police in her bedroom drawer with the words, 'You'll regret the day you were ever born!' scrawled in red marker, paints a much different picture! In Camille's sick head, if Phil couldn't see that they belonged together, then he deserved to die. She had it all planned out, Phil La Paglia was going to meet his maker the night of the St. Francis dance. She brought the poisoned bottle of Jim Beam with her in her purse, and substituted the bourbon when she first took over the bar on Stanley's bathroom break. By the time Stanley poured Phil his first drink, his fate was sealed. The police didn't find the Jim Beam bottle or any Belladonna plants in Camille's apartment, so she must have disposed of those. However, they were able to find receipts, proving the plants had been billed and shipped to her address, a few days prior to the dance." Arianna stopped at Camille's chair, and rather obnoxiously, leaned in and got right in her face. "Sloppy sloppy Camille! Haven't you ever heard of using a P.O. Box?"

"Fongool!" Camille spat out, while simultaneously using a rude hand gesture to accentuate her point.

"Hey, watch it bitch!" Sallie leapt to Arianna's defense and started pummeling Camille in the chest, while Camille attempted to protect herself by trying to scratching Sallie's eyes out. Unfortunately, Stanley could be of no assistance. He had been snoring loudly during the last couple minutes of the proceedings and had just been rudely awakened by all the commotion. Sadly, Stanley was also experiencing a huge panic attack, because he couldn't remember where he was and didn't know why so many people were in his bedroom.

Mike stepped in quickly. "Hey, hey, cool it! Sallie, get out of here. And you, you shut your mouth!" he angrily told Camille, grabbing her wrists and cuffing her.

Sandra shook her head and clucked, "Tsk tsk, as I've said before, the Italians have no control over their temper."

"You're one to talk Mom. Hit someone over the head with a wine bottle lately?" Arianna retorted, admittingly taking delight in watching Sandra's face turn an extremely bright shade of red.

Mike led Camille outside, where he had considerately made sure there was police backup waiting. Soon after, the three ladies, Sarah, Rachel and Esther walked past them all and left the church, too busy talking animatedly amongst themselves, to pay any attention to Arianna. Arlene did make a point of stopping by with Paula, before they left, and hugged her. "Thank you, Riann for bringing Phil's killer to justice and giving us the great news about Stanley. We will definitely be contacting him later, and I want you to know you're welcome in my home anytime."

"Oh thank you! Do you think I could borrow your butler sometime?" Arianna looked hopeful.

"We'll see," she said, smiling in response.

Paula looked down at her shoes and quickly mumbled, "thank you," before walking outside with her mother.

Sandra and Barry came by next. "Well done dear, although I do sometimes wish you had a 'normal' hobby," her mother told her. Arianna made a face.

Barry nodded at Arianna. "Yeah, uh way to go, real exciting stuff there," he said. He hooked arms with Sandra and said, "Whaddya say we blow this Popsicle stand, dollface?" Sandra, smiling, nodded her assent while Arianna groaned loudly.

A much calmer Stanley (Sandra had considerately filled him in on his current location) walked over to her. "Thank you sweetheart," he said, patting Arianna on the shoulder, "and please thank your boyfriend for me as well, I hope he's doing better." He winked knowingly at her. Arianna shot a frustrated look at Sallie.

Sallie gave Arianna a big hug and cried, "Riann, that was so exciting, I knew you could do it! I'm so glad you cleared my Stanley's name. I just wish Mike would have let me continue to beat that bitch's ass. How dare she insult you like that! If it wasn't for her, you might have married Phil and had kids, and if I marry Stanley, I could have been a grandmother to your kids!" she whined.

"Ummm right," Arianna replied, rolling her eyes. "Don't worry Sallie, Camille will receive more than enough punishment in prison. Thank you so much for all your help, and good luck in your uh, relationship."

Sallie said, "No problem, but dang it, I was so sure it was Esther. I do think I would have felt differently though if I had been able to meet with both Esther and Camille. I'm sure I 'd have received some psychic impression that Camille was 'off.'"

Suddenly, Sallie lowered her voice and leaned in closer to her. "I do want to tell you something privately though." She drew Arianna off to the side and looked furtively over to her left and right before she started speaking. "I wanted to tell you, I am picking up something really strong about you and Mike. Your relationship will be getting MUCH more serious."

"Oh?" Arianna replied, trying not to appear too excited.

She winked and said, "Mike's been thinking about you all the time lately, you know. He's totally in love with you, Riann. You both will be getting all hot and heavy again very soon and everything will be BETTER THAN EVER in the bedroom..."

Arianna blushed, and for once in her life, had nothing to say.

Epilogue

A month later, Arianna Archer walked into the Meadowville police station accompanied by a woman with light brown, fashionably cut hair, and sparkling blue eyes, accentuated by long black lashes. The woman was wearing a light coat of pink blush on her cheeks and frosted pink lipstick and her recently manicured fingernails were painted a lovely shade of coral red. She was dressed in a mauve, knee-length, designer dress with a purple belt and white, low-heeled, open-toed shoes. "Come this way," Arianna told her, and led her through the maze of desks over to Mike Stevenson's office.

As they walked by, all the other policemen yelled out, "Hi Riann!" and looked curiously at her companion.

Arianna returned their greetings and then knocked on Mike's door. He mumbled, "Come in," not looking up at all, as he was deeply engrossed in a bunch of paperwork. They walked inside and his face immediately brightened. "Hi Riann, nice to see you," he said. Mike glanced over at the other woman and appeared puzzled. He stood up, stepped out from behind his desk over to her and introduced himself. "Hello, I'm Mike, I don't think we've ever met before," he said, extending his hand. The woman shook his hand and grinned.

"I told you!" Arianna declared triumphantly to her.

"Told her what?" he looked at both of them quizzically.

Grinning mischievously, Arianna said, "I told her that you wouldn't recognize her. This is Paula."

"Paula?" he asked.

"Paula La Paglia," the other woman interjected.

"Paula La Paglia?" His eyes widened. "Oh wow, I apologize. I didn't recognize you. It's just that you look so so…"

"Good?" Paula asked, smiling.

"Different, I was going to say, but good will do. You look great!"

Paula blushed and Arianna explained, "We gave Paula a makeover at my house. I sicced the Archer ladies on her, and I have to say, they did a marvelous job!"

"They did do a marvelous job, and I'm so grateful!" Paula squeezed Arianna's hand. "Her mother also gave me a stern talking to about wasting my life, and lectured me on how I deserve to be happy and have someone to love me. She's even going to take me to the next St. Francis Singles Dance."

"Better you than me," declared Arianna cheerfully.

"That is fantastic," Mike said sincerely. "Actually, I'm glad you came by Riann. Ed told me he was so pleased with the results of the St. Francis investigation that he wants to hire you as a full-time consultant. Would you be interested?" he asked her smiling, knowing full well what her answer would be.

Arianna almost began jumping up and down, she was so excited, but managed to restrain herself. "Oh my God, how totally awesome!" She had been worrying lately about making her next mortgage payment, so this job offer came just in time.

"You can come in tomorrow at 9:00 am and ask to see Ed. He'll go over all the details with you," Mike told her.

Paula said, "That's terrific Riann, I'm happy for you."

"Thanks!" she replied, grinning from ear to ear.

"Well, should we go now?" Paula asked.

"You can go," she answered. "I think I'll stay here for a bit." Paula nodded and left Mike's office.

Arianna looked at Mike. "We took separate cars here," she explained.

Mike praised her, "Great job with Paula, Riann. I know that must have been quite the project."

"It certainly was, but miraculous things can happen once a person starts to feel good about themselves."

"Amen to that," he agreed.

"She's actually going to go to dinner with Stanley and Sallie tonight," Arianna informed him.

"No kidding!"

"Yeah, Sallie was so happy that Stanley now had a granddaughter, that they've been spending tons of time with Paula. It's funny watching Sallie try to be a grandmother to someone almost her exact age."

"I'm sure," he replied, chuckling.

"But Paula seems to genuinely like hanging out with them, and vice-versa. They've made a big impact on her. She's even been motivated to clean her house, thank God!"

"That's incredible," he said, leaning back against his desk.

Arianna looked down at the floor and, not realizing that her face had already betrayed her, nonchalantly asked, "So, how is Barbara doing?" It was quite obvious that she cared very much what his response would be.

Mike sighed. "Listen Riann, I wanted to tell you before but I was obligated not to. Barbara had come over to my house that night for professional advice."

"Professional advice? I don't understand."

"Barbara was coming over to ask for advice on matters concerning her husband," he explained.

"Concerning Carlos?" Arianna asked, surprised.

"Don't you read the papers?" he asked her, tossing yesterday's "Somerset Hills Gazette" at her. Arianna assumed his question was merely rhetorical. Mike was well aware that she only got her news from the TV show, The Colbert Report.

Smack in the middle of the front page was a big picture of Barbara's husband and the headline above it read, "Drug Cartel Kingpin Busted!" She turned to the first page. "Local businessman, Carlos Izquierda, was taken into custody yesterday, after the police, working side by side with drug enforcement, were able to collect enough evidence to prove Izquierda is a leader of a prominent Latin American drug cartel."

Mike said, "Over a year ago, Barbara had tipped off the Somerset Hills police that she suspected her husband of running a drug operation. She had stumbled onto a large amount of cash and his explanation of what it was and why he had it did not add up. The Somerset Hills police began working with the DEA to try and bring him down. That cop Tom, the one you saw me talking with at the wake, was one of the cops in charge of the investigation. I can't go into specific details, but Barbara had a few concerns for her safety that she wanted to discuss with me. She also had some questions about my experiences testifying in these types of cases when they go to trial."

"Really? That's great!" Arianna couldn't hide the joy and relief she felt. "I, I mean, how awful for her," she attempted to appear somber.

"I know, I don't envy her one bit," Mike replied gravely.

"Couldn't you have just told me all this, when I first asked you?"

"Riann, that would have been a severe violation of Barbara's privacy. There was also an ongoing DEA investigation, that hadn't been wrapped up yet, to consider. Do you know what would have happened to me if I had leaked this information to you?"

"No, what?" Arianna's big green eyes widened.

"The DEA would have made sure that I did hard time in Cook County Jail."

"Cook County Jail?!" she cried out in alarm.

Mike saw the look on her face and chuckled, "Boy, you believe anything, don't you?"

She gave him a dirty look and swatted him on the arm. "Well, that mystery's solved, at least. By the way, do you know if Carlos owns a recreational vehicle?"

"I have no idea, why?" he asked her.

"Maybe he's not just a druglord, but cooks meth as well," she suggested.

Puzzled, Mike asked, "Cooks meth? What would give you the idea that he cooks meth?"

Arianna, mildly annoyed, looked at him. "Breaking Bad of course!"

"Oh, of course," he replied, rolling his eyes. "No, I don't believe he's 'Walter White'."

"Yay, you know who Walter White is!" she happily exclaimed. "Wow, this is all pretty unbelievable. All I can say is Barbara must have really bad taste in men," she teased him.

"Ha, ha, very funny," Mike said, while Arianna grinned.

After a few seconds of silence, she said softly, "You know, I thought you and Barbara were sleeping together."

"Riann, you ninny, you know I don't have that type of feeling for her anymore, and vice-versa. I can't believe you would think that."

She gave him an embarrassed look. "Well you know, she's so sophisticated and educated and everything, and so, so thin," she blurted out.

"You silly goose, don't I always tell you I love your curves?"

"Yeah, but Barbara's always been skinny and you married her, so you must like skinny women," she reasoned.

"I was too young to know what I wanted back then," Mike told her, laying his hand upon her left shoulder.

"I also noticed that you never say anything negative about her at all, and I started to think that maybe it's because you still have a thing for her," she explained, feeling ashamed of herself.

"The reason I don't badmouth her, is because I respect her. It's my belief, that if you have a marriage or a long-term relationship with somebody, if it was real love that love wouldn't turn into indifference or hate when the relationship is severed. Real love is permanent and unconditional. I'll always feel love for Barbara, but I'll never be in love with her again, does that make sense?"

Arianna was quiet for a moment. "I get it. Thank you for explaining it to me. Hey, would you like to come over for dinner tonight?"

"Dinner? I'd love to, what time?"

Arianna replied, "How about seven? I'm making beef teriyaki, so bring your appetite."

"Really, beef teriyaki? What's got into you, why are you a domestic goddess all of a sudden?"

"Hey, I'm not that bad in the kitchen," she, not very convincingly, defended herself.

"Well, I can hardly wait," he told her, walking her to the door.

"Oh, and Mike…, bring an overnight bag," she said, smiling mischievously as she walked out of his office, leaving him grinning in her wake.

The End

ABOUT THE AUTHOR

Karen Berg-Raftakis is a die-hard murder mystery fan. She has a B.A. in English from The University of Illinois at Chicago, and lives in Brookfield, Illinois with her family and two cats. She is the author of Murder on the Church Council and is hard at work on the third book of her Arianna Archer murder mystery series.